Manning the LIGHT

*For the keepers
of the Rose Island
Lighthouse*

Manning the
LIGHT

Terry Webb

TERRY
WEBB

Pleasant Word
A Division of WINEPRESS PUBLISHING

Illustrations by: Karla Cochran

Printed in the United States of America

Packaged by Pleasant Word, a division of WinePress Publishing, PO Box 428, Enumclaw, WA 98022. The views expressed or implied in this work do not necessarily reflect those of Pleasant Word, a division of WinePress Publishing. Ultimate design, content, and editorial accuracy of this work are the responsibilities of the author.

Unless otherwise noted, all Scriptures are taken from the Holy Bible, New International Version, Copyright © 1973, 1978, 1984 by the International Bible Society. Used by permission of Zondervan Publishing House.

ISBN 1-57921-669-2
Library of Congress Catalog Card Number: 2003105341

Dedication

This story is dedicated to:

Chris, Molly, Charlie, Ben, Matthew, Billy, Rachel, William, Lucy, Daniel, Evan, and Alexandra

Table of Contents

Acknowledgment

I wish to acknowledge the invaluable assistance of the Maine Maritime Museum, in Bath, Maine, especially Susan Russell and Nathan R. Lipfert, who researched the boats commonly used by lighthouse keepers and the Lighthouse Service Board in 1903. Elaine Jones, the educational specialist for the State of Maine and curator for the Burnt Island lighthouse in Boothbay Harbor, Maine, provided expert advice on the life of lighthouse families who lived on islands. Barbara Skinner Rumsey, librarian at the Boothbay Harbor Historical Society, helped with dialect expressions of Maine seamen and sailors. I also wish to thank Beth Griner and my grandchildren who read and critiqued the story.

CHAPTER 1

The Job

That ringing!

"Help!" A voice called.

"Coming, Pa!" His feet were like lead. He couldn't get started. Grief gripped him.

Louie sat bolt upright, his body in a cold sweat. That dream. It kept returning, night after night. The ringing stopped and he opened his eyes. Over the iron bedposts he saw his mother rummaging through her opened trunk. He lay back down, catching the sob in his throat, then he pulled the quilt over his head.

"That's the last breakfast bell."

He heard Ma's muffled voice through the quilt. She pulled the quilt back and shook him gently.

"This is our big day."

He opened one eye to watch her. She placed his trousers, suspenders, shirt, and jacket at the foot of his bed and then disappeared down the hall with her clothes over her arm.

They were staying at the Backbay Boarding House in town up the road from the office of the U.S. Lighthouse Service Board. Louie, still tired from the long train ride the day before, rubbed the sleep from his eyes. He missed Pa.

He pulled up the trousers. This time they reached only to below his knees. He must have grown six inches since he'd worn them at the funeral. Even then they were too short. Ma had told him they couldn't afford to buy new ones. He would have to wear them until she could find a job.

A job. Ma never had to worry about a job before when his pa and grandpa were alive. They were a family then. Now they had to help each other, just the two of them.

"Can't I wear my overalls, Ma?" he pleaded when she returned from the washroom, "These make me look stupid!"

"You'll feel better once we've had breakfast and the interview is over."

He sighed and followed her down the stairs. As soon as he smelled the fresh blueberry muffins and steaming oatmeal, he forgot about everything except filling his stomach.

An hour later Louie stood behind his mother as she knocked on the door of the Lighthouse Service Board office. He heard the rustling of papers and the scrape of a chair. The door opened and a mustached man in a dark blue jacket ushered them in. Rays of bright morning sunlight streaming from a nearby window bounced off his bald head. The supervisor pointed to two chairs in front of his desk.

"Good morning, Mr. McAllister—"

"Please—take a seat."

Louie wasn't sure who had spoken first, his mother or the supervisor.

Louie waited until Ma sat down; then, following her lead, he sat on the chair beside her. He folded and unfolded his hands and shuffled his feet under the chair.

Mr. McAllister scratched his head, then his nose. "Ah-Ah-Ah-Choo."

"Get that feather away from my nose!" He reached into his shirt pocket for a handkerchief.

Louie's mother took off her feathered hat and put it in her lap. Louie had told her she looked like a peacock in that hat and tried to talk her out of wearing it, but she put it on anyway.

Mr. McAllister sneezed again.

Louie bent over, took the hat from his mother's lap and held it with one hand behind his chair.

She stiffened and balanced on the edge of her chair.

"My name is Molly Hollander. I've come to apply for the job as the lighthouse keeper on Two Tree Island in Windlass Bay. This is my son, Louie."

Louie moved the hat from one hand to another as Mr. McAllister swivelled back in his chair. He watched the superintendent's eyes as they moved from his mother's high-necked collar to her red cape down to her high-heeled boots. Next, Louie felt those eyes boring through him. Taking his free hand he combed his unruly dark brown hair with his fingers away from his own hazel eyes. He tried to fold up his lanky frame. His feet would not stop shuffling.

"No!" Mr. McAllister stroked his bald spot. "Lighthouse tending is hard, dangerous work and we don't hire women unless they come along with a strong man."

"That hat and that cape," he shook his head, "the first wind will blow it off and that red cape will nevah keep you warm and dry on stormy days."

"Why? I'm used to working around lighthouses—" Louie's mother replied. Louie looked up as the officer interrupted.

"It takes one or two strong men to tend the lighthouses along this coast."

Louie's mother rested her hand on Louie's shoulder.

"My son will work alongside me. He's very strong. He helped my husband and me tend the lighthouse on Swanton Point."

Unable to fold up Louie slouched down in his chair. He kept his eyes on the floor.

No one spoke for what seemed like hours. Mr. McAllister sat back in his chair, drummed his fingers on the oak desk, then stroked his head and his mustache.

"Well . . . I need someone to take over tending Two Tree Island Light. The keeper brought his family but his wife didn't like the loneliness of living on that island. His kids complained because they had no othah children to play with them. They have moved to the mainland but the keeper has had to stay on the island until we find his replacement."

Mr. McAllister leaned over the desk and asked Louie, "How old are you, boy?"

Louie stopped shuffling his feet. He felt the pink move up from his neck to his checks. He sat up tall.

"I'm thirteen, going on fourteen and my name is Louie, Sir."

Louie spoke with more confidence than he felt. He really just had his thirteenth birthday. But going on fourteen sounded better than thirteen now that he was supposed to be the man of the family.

"My pa was a lighthouse keeper. So were my grandpas. I know all about lighthouse tending."

"He has many talents," Ma added.

"We work together just as we did with his pa and my pa." She reached over to hold Louie's hand.

"Do you know how to warn ships when they are close to the rocks? Can you tend the lamps in stormy weather?" Mr. McAllister asked Louie's mother.

Louie squirmed in his chair.

Here she goes again. He sighed.

Louie's mother sat back in her chair.

"I've lived in lighthouses since I was a little girl. During one winter storm the waves broke over our whole island, flooded our house, and broke all the windows. My pa moved us to the lighthouse tower so that we could still keep the lamps blazing during the storm. When he left us to rescue some of our household goods, he was washed out to sea."

"We stayed in the lighthouse tower and kept the lamps lit all night, even when the waves kept lashing the tower. We saved two ships from crashing against our rocks in that bad storm."

Louie had heard her tell the story many times.

She continued, "Now will you hire us?"

"Well . . ." Mr. McAllister again sat back in his chair. He scratched his bald spot and then stroked his mustache.

"I really need to send someone out to tend that light," he said.

"Just give us a chance," Ma pleaded.

Louie nodded. She continued.

"My husband died five months ago and we need the money."

She took out her lace handkerchief and held it up to her eyes. Louie squeezed the hat and clenched his other hand into a fist.

Louie mumbled to himself, would this man ever make up his mind?

Mr. McAllister replied as if he heard.

"All right." He sighed. "You'll have to do until I can hire a regulah man."

Louie slumped in his chair and looked down at the floor again.

Lighthouse Service Board: A nine-member Board created by Congress in 1852 to oversee servicing all the U.S. lighthouses. The country was divided into twelve districts, with an inspector—a naval officer or district engineer—for each. The local customs collector, a political appointee, was the district supervisor.

CHAPTER 2

Defining the Job

Y ou can have the job—at least temporarily."

Mr. McAllister pulled out a paper from his drawer. "Your salary will be forty-five dollahs a month. Here's your July wages in advance so you can buy rubber boots and oilskin jackets, if you don't have them, and any provisions you need. I'll take you both to Jake's store when you're ready and help you set up an account. You'll have thirty days vacation whenever a man lighthouse keepah can relieve you."

Does he have to rub it in again? Louie thought as he shrank deeper in his chair.

Mr. McAllister handed Louie's mother some papers to sign. Louie unclenched his fist. Finally, he thought.

Then Mr. McAllister walked over to a cupboard in the corner of the room and took out two blue jackets with brass buttons like his and two keepers' hats with the Lighthouse Board shield on them."

"Here's your uniforms. We make our rounds about once every three months of all the lighthouses, weather permitting. A gundalow scowl will bring your coal toward fall. *Isleshore Service* operates a mission for folks who live out on islands all year round.

Their ship, *Rainbow*, makes rounds when she tends buoys. Captain Bowline can stop at Two Tree Island if you need him."

"Son . . ."

My name's Louie and you're not my pa! Louie almost blurted out and then clamped his mouth tight. He did not want to cause Ma to lose the job.

". . . will you be coming to the mainland for school in Septembah?"

At Swanton Point, when Louie's pa was still alive, Louie took the bus every day to the town's school, at least every day he could.

Mr. McAllister turned to Mrs. Hollander.

"We can arrange to have the *Rainbow* pick him up on Monday and return him on Friday, weather permitting of course."

"No, thank you. I need him to help keep the lighthouse."

Louie nodded. They had talked it over—at least Ma had pointed out that she needed him to help her. If she got the job, Louie had agreed to continue his schooling on the island.

"Then the *Rainbow* will bring a library box of lesson books and assignments in Septembah. One of our retired teachers has agreed to be a visiting teacher to oversee the learning of island children who can't make it to the mainland for one reason or other. During the summer months a visiting preacher makes rounds, too. A nurse is available when you need her."

Louie watched as Ma read the contract. She dipped the fountain pen into the ink well and signed the papers. Then she handed Louie the two jackets and hats. He managed to juggle his new load with the feathered hat and pick up Ma's red cape on the back of her chair while standing up. Meanwhile, she was shaking Mr. McAllister's hand.

"Our trunks are just down the road at the boarding house. We will go back and change these clothes into our working uniforms.

It will only take us an hour. Will you pick us up and take us to Jake's store?"

Mr. McAllister agreed, then escorted them both to the door. The red cape trailed behind Louie as he bolted through the door after Ma, mumbling a "thank you."

"Pick up that cape off the ground, Louie. You know how special it is to me! Here, I'll wear it."

Louie gave Ma back the red cape and dutifully followed her down the path to the boarding house.

Although he still seethed over some of Mr. McAllister's comments, Louie had no doubt that he and his ma could handle their new job just like men. Little did he realize the dangers that life on their new island home would bring.

Bowline: A type of knot used to tie a ship to a piling or mooring. It is a knot which never slips or jams and has many uses at sea.

Gundalow: A flat bottomed scowl sloop-type boat, like a freighter, used to bring coal to island lighthouses.

CHAPTER 3

Ready—Get Set

He let her hug him.

As Ma did so she mumbled in his ear, "I was proud of you this morning." Seeing the other boarders watching, Louie broke loose and ran upstairs to change into his overalls.

"Can I throw out these town clothes that don't fit now you got the job?" was the first thing out of Louie's mouth as he pulled on his comfortable new overalls.

"No," replied Ma, "you're still growing. We'll wait until we come into town on the first shore leave for new town clothes. I used the last of our savings to buy you those new work shoes and overalls. Now, we need to buy provisions with this and next month's wages."

Louie didn't want to wait. She had promised that if she got the job he could have new town clothes.

"But these are kids' clothes . . ."

Ma put her fingers to his lips.

His thoughts wandered back to the last Christmas they'd had together with Pa. Pa had waited to give Ma her present until Louie had opened all of his. Pa watched Ma lovingly when she carefully opened the box and took out the red cape.

"How beautiful!" Ma exclaimed as she held the cape close to her chest. Then she had given Pa a smaller box. Inside was a brass barometer for predicting the weather. On it were the words: STORMY, RAIN, CHANGE, FAIR, VERY DRY. He remembered Pa putting his fingers to his lips and blowing her a kiss.

Louie came back abruptly to now.

"Gosh darn!"

He threw the too-tight-and-short town clothes on his brass bed along with the uniforms. Then, he collected the rest of his stuff scattered around the room. As he tossed them into his trunk he spied the brass barometer. Ma had given it to him after the funeral. Some of his Pa's old clothes were there—for him to grow into.

Louie flopped onto the brass bed and wept into the pillow. Ma stopped her packing and sat beside him.

She had told him after the funeral that he was the man of the family now. But he didn't feel like a man because he still wore kids' clothes that didn't fit anymore. Maybe . . . if he could only wear mens' clothes.

He lifted his head. There beside him lay the new double breasted dark blue jacket with the brass buttons on the bed. Ma handed him her lace handkerchief. Louie wiped away the tears, blew his nose and sat up.

Carefully, he slipped the sleeves of the new jacket over his arms and buttoned the jacket. Standing in front of the round mirror above the dresser, he admired his new self. Other than the sleeves being too long, at least it was a man's jacket.

"Okay!" He stood up to his full height.

Ma retrieved her everyday skirt and blouse from the depths of her trunk and carefully folded her red cape. She placed it in the trunk with her feather hat on top. Then she, too, put on a jacket with the brass buttons over her blouse. She came over to the dresser and stood beside Louie.

"We make quite a team," she said putting her arm around Louie.

Louie carried their trunks downstairs to the parlor.

Outside, a wagon had pulled up in front of the boarding house and the driver stepped down.

"Mrs. Hollander?" he asked.

"That's my name."

"Where's Mr. McAllister?" asked Louie.

"He's waiting at Jake's store. Asked me to fetch ye. Name's Aussie."

Aussie heaved their two trunks onto the wagon and drove them with Louie and his mother sitting up front to the store.

Four men smoking cigars were sitting talking around a potbellied stove in the middle of the front room of the store.

"Ayuh, Ms. Hollander," one of them said. "Heard ye was the new lighthouse keeper over at Two Tree Island." The other three blew smoke toward Louie's mother.

Phew! thought Louie as he tried to wave the smoky air away. The cigar smoke in the room choked him and he didn't like the smell. He took his mother's arm and dragged her over toward the counter.

With his back to the men, Louie could now look around the store. Shelves holding canned goods, bolts of cloth, and yarn lined the walls behind a counter. Barrels sat in corners and fishing supplies, notions and needles, and packages of seeds covered every inch of the rest of the space.

After Ma had selected the cans of food and some bolts of cloth she wanted, Louie helped her put them in boxes along with bags of flour, corn meal, and other staples, enough to last for a week.

"I've already opened your account with your first month's wages," Mr. McAllister's voice came from behind them.

"You can order against next month's wages, too. Jake can get you anything you need."

Jake grinned, chawed his tobacco, and turned to spit in the spittoon near him. He brushed his long locks of hair back from his forehead and wiped his hands on his dirty apron.

"Anything else ye be need'n, Mrs. Hollander?"

Jake leaned over the counter.

"I've got catalogs here, livestock and household stuff in the shed."

He took them through a side door and out to a shed behind the store. Squawking roosters, hens, and chickens ran between assorted chairs, tables, bed stands, and stoves. Barrels of feed and containers filled the corners. Behind the shed horses and cows were tethered. A few pigs wandered around. Ma picked out two hens and a rooster and ordered a dairy cow with feed to be bought out on the *Rainbow*. She spied a treadle sewing machine among the tables.

"I'll buy that, too, on next month's wages," she told Jake.

"You can send it out with the cow and the bolts of cloth."

Louie selected boys' magazines and a few fishing hooks while his mother completed her purchases.

"Don't forget those rubber boots and foul weather jackets," reminded their new boss, pointing to one side of the store. Louie looked and saw oil skin jackets on a rack, boots and galoshes underneath.

"Oh—thanks for reminding me," Ma said.

Louie and Ma found two pairs of boots and oilskin jackets that seemed to be the right fit. Louie placed them on top of their pile of boxes and bags. Jake gave them some oil cloth to put around the boxes during the crossing.

"Can I have that pocket knife, too?" Louie pleaded. "The pocket knife you and Pa gave me is rusted. I have a hard time opening it."

Ma nodded her head, yes. Louie forgot all about the new clothes he had wanted earlier.

"We'll have to hurry," cautioned Mr. McAllister.

"The tide's changing and we want to get you settled before sundown. It's quite a fur piece to the island. We have to row two dories across because the lighthouse tender doesn't run today."

The loaded wagon bounced along over the rutted road to the town wharf. Louie held on tight to the cages with the two hens and a rooster. He expected to see either one of the boxes of canned goods or a trunk fly off. But they all made it safely to the wharf where two dories waited to ferry them to the island.

———————————

Lighthouse Keeper: Someone hired by the Lighthouse Service Board to take care of a lighthouse. Mostly they were men but women were lighthouse keepers as early as 1768. Keeping a lighthouse was also called tending a lighthouse beacon or manning a light house beacon.

Dory: A flat bottomed boat with a squared stern and a rounded bow, used for rowing people, supplies, and catching fish. It could be anywhere from 16 to 24 feet long. A dory was more difficult to row than a double-ender.

Double-ender: A round bottomed boat with a pointed bow and stern that had two middle seats. They were found at lighthouses and used as lifeboats or for fishing; also used to ferry people and supplies from larger vessels to shore and visa-versa. They could be as long as 16 ft. After 1915, these boats were called peapods.

Wharf: A waterfront construction for mooring vessels for the purposes of safe loading, outfitting, maintenance, and repair of boats. A wharf can be a pier built out into the water so as to enable vessels to be moored alongside.

Tender: A large steam powered vessel used by the Lighthouse Service Board to carry supplies to lighthouses.

CHAPTER 4

GO

Let me help you, Ma'am."

Mr. McAllister took Louie's mother's arm and guided her as she stepped into the first dory. Louie followed holding a cage in each hand. Two sailors managed to squeeze two boxes with provisions in with them and covered them all with oil cloth. Then they loaded another dory with the trunks, a can of feed, and Mr. McAllister.

"Stroke, together. Stroke." The men rowed out toward the islands in the distance.

"Better put those jackets on," Mr. McAllister hollered from the other dory. "She's breezing up and it's rough out here!"

The oarsmen fought both wind and waves. It took the dories two hours to cover the mile from the town wharf to Two Tree Island. Louie sat in the bow and licked the salt spray off his cheeks and lips. The hens and rooster in their cages at his feet made a loud protest to the spraying water dampening their feathers.

Louie's dory reached the island first. The oarsmen made several attempts to bring her close to a short pier jutting out at the base of a rock cliff.

A tramway ran beside the pier up to a shed nestled in the rock Louie could see steps cut into the rocks winding up the rock face to a lighthouse complex on top. A cresting wave brought them close enough to slip the ship's painters around the pilings and their oarsman to jump off onto the small pier. Meanwhile a man in a keeper's hat and jacket came down the steps and started an engine in the shed. The seaman guided the dory around to the tramway and hooked the steel cable to the bow.

"Ready," he yelled above the noise of the pounding surf.

"Squawk! Squawk!" Louie put his hands over the foul cages to calm the hens and rooster as the engine winched up their dory until it was above the breaking water. Louie helped Ma out of the boat and the seaman unloaded their boxes.

"Ye must be the missus," the keeper shouted above the screeching wind. "This here yer son?"

"Where's the new keeper?"

"I am." Louie's mother shouted back.

The keeper's mouth dropped.

"Ayuh?"

Their seaman motioned the keeper to lower the dory so Mr. McAllister's dory and their trunks could land. The oarsman in the second dory hooked the steel cable to the bow. Mr. McAllister stepped out of the dory and the seaman unloaded their trunks and the rest of the provisions.

"Watch yer step, Ma'am. Them stairs are steep and slippery," cautioned the seaman. Louie gave the bird cages to his mother and turned to help the keeper, Mr. McAllister, and the sailor take their boxes and trunks up to house on top of the rock cliff.

After their trunks and boxes had been deposited by the front steps of the house, the keeper handed Louie's mother a pamphlet.

"Here's the instructions for manning the light, Ma'am."

He turned to ask Mr. McAllister.

"Shall I show 'em around?"

Mr. McAllister took off his hat, wiped his bald head, and stroked his mustache.

"Don't have time. Need to be getting back before dark."

Both men tipped their hats to Ma as they started back down the winding steps.

Mr. McAllister said, "You'll find some kerosene for your lamps in the oil shed and coal for your stove in the work shed. If you need any other supplies, you can tell the captain of the *Rainbow* when she comes round tomorrow,"

He glanced over at the tower.

"Looks like that tower could use some touch up. I'll send over some paint and brushes."

Louie followed the two men down the steps to the waiting dory. The keeper gave a box to the waiting seaman along with his duffel and eagerly climbed aboard the dory.

"Oh, almost forgot, Son." Mr. McAllister stopped and turned around to Louie who stood behind him.

"There's a double-ender in that shed over thah. It's for rescuing at sea, but you can use it for rowing and fishing when the seas calm down some."

Fine, Louie thought, but I wish he'd stop calling me son! He couldn't wait for Mr. McAllister to get back in the boat.

"Hurry," he said instead.

"Tide's turning."

Mr. McAllister had barely made it into the dory behind the keeper before Louie had loosened the winch holding the cable. The dory went down the tramway so fast Mr. McAllister literally fell into his seat. It made a big splash when it made contact with the water.

"Next time a littler slower—boy," Mr. McAllister shouted while the oarsmen rowed away just as the sun began to set.

Oarsman: The person who rows the boat with oars.

Stroke together stroke: means dipping both oars in the water at the same time and pulling them through the water.

Ayuh: A New England way of expressing agreement or surprise. Dialogue in this story has other regional dialect expressions.

Tramway: Wooden or metal tracks running from sea to boat shed or house. Often called slip.

Pier: Sometimes made of stone or brick to hold up a wharf.

Painter: A line tied to the bow of a boat that is used to fasten the boat to a dock, pier, or wharf.

Piling (or pile): Vertical wooden (often oak) pole pounded into sea or river bed to hold up a wharf.

Tide: Created by the gravitational pull of the sun and the moon. A coming or rising tide is when the surface of the ocean against a shore line rises; an ebbing tide is when the surface of the ocean drops. The movement of the tide from high to low occurs twice a day.

CHAPTER 5

Moving in

T hat man . . .," Louie muttered.

He clenched and unclenched his smarting hands. Big ugly blisters had formed from letting the cable run through his hands so fast.

He climbed back up the steps, ignoring the waiting pile of boxes, trunks, and cages. Instead, he gazed at their new house. It had gabled windows and attached shutters. A long shed was attached to one side of the house and connected to a three story circular stone and brick tower base. The lighthouse beacon was on top. Placed helter-skelter at other spots around the island were other sheds. One conical one stood like a metronome close to the lighthouse.

"That must be the fog bell," said Louie pointing it out to Ma, "and that other brick one an oil house. Have to investigate those others."

Meanwhile, Louie's mother seemed absorbed in her own thoughts.

"This is the day we begin our new service. We'll have to man this lighthouse without your pa. Think we can manage?"

She turned. Louie was already half way down the hill exploring the shed with the double-ender and running his hands around its gunwales.

"Sure, Ma!" Louie called up to her, not as optimistic as he sounded.

"How soon can I row her?" he asked, turning back to the boat with its round bottom and two pointed ends.

"Remember our first responsibility, Louie; rowing will come later. We have to keep the lamp burning," she reminded him.

"As soon as we carry our trunks, these boxes, bags and cages into the house, we'll need to fill the lamp with kerosene, light the wicks, and clean the windows and the lens in the lighthouse tower before it gets dark."

Ma opened the door to the house and the two of them put all their belongings safely inside. Ma opened the door to the outside of the lighthouse tower and they climbed the winding stairs.

"A Fresnel lens!" exclaimed Louie with delight." Not the old fashioned Argand lamps we had on Swanton Point. I hated cleaning and lighting them in the winter. And it doesn't use that expensive whale oil. We had to heat it every time to soften it so it would wick up."

The Fresnel lamp jet needed cleaning and the 4th-order lenses dusted and polished. Even the windows of the lighthouse were sooty. Louie took a bucket and rag and went out on the catwalk that surrounded the tower to clean the outside of the windows while his mother worked on the inside. Then Louie went to the brick oil house and filled a fresh can with kerosene. Ma lit the lamp and checked to see if a spare lamp was ready in case the wicks went out or smoked up. Louie took a special polishing cloth and wiped all the soot and smudges off the prisms until they shined. He remembered to pick the right silk cloth, not a cotton one because cotton would leave scratches on the lens. They finished just as the sun set and the sky turned dark.

Ma lit a kerosene lamp they found in the work shed that connected to the tower. Louie could make out in the shadows a bin and some coal chunks on the dirt floor along with tools scattered around.

The keeper must have forgotten to put these away, he thought.

Next, they let the hens and rooster out of their cages, gave them some feed, and showed them some racks in the shed where they could sleep. Finally, they were ready to explore the inside of their new home.

A parlor, kitchen, and two bedrooms took up the first floor space. An outdoor walkway led to a small outhouse in the rear of the house. With the lamp held high, they looked into one bedroom and saw two iron beds with ropes lashed across the frames. Their corn-husk mattresses lay propped up beside them and against the wall stood a tall chest of drawers.

"Ugh!" exclaimed Louie. "I liked our house on Swanton Point better."

Louie's mother ignored his distaste.

"We'll wait 'till tomorrow to explore the dormered loft and unpack. Those stairs are too narrow and we can't see well with this lamp."

Louie shivered—remembering.

Or someone else falling, he thought.

They found another lamp and Louie lit the wick. In the kitchen, they noted unwashed dishes piled in the wooden sink and a coffee pot and some pans on the black pot-bellied iron stove.

"You can tell the last lighthouse keeper didn't have his wife here to take good care of this house." Ma sighed, "Or he didn't have time to wash these before we arrived."

"We'll start tidying up tomorrow."

Louie put the lamp on a table while Ma opened a can of beans. They managed to collect two quilts and pillows from their trunks. After placing the two mattresses back up on their rope beds, they crawled under the quilts.

Louie yawned. "I wish Pa were here."

"I do, too, but we have this job and a home to live in. We can keep on just as he would want us to."

Louie swallowed the sob at the back of his throat.

"Your pa taught us just to trust in God and he would protect us even through the worst of the storms."

"But he didn't protect Pa!" Louie started crying. Louie put his head on Ma's shoulder. She held him and stroked his head just as she had when he was a little boy.

"But see, he's taking care of us now. We have a new lighthouse to live in and a new light to tend."

She started praying the familiar prayer. "Our Father . . . Louie joined in. She ended with, "We thank you for this job and your protection, Lord. Amen."

Louie pulled the quilt up to his chin. He thought he heard the now familiar sound of his pa calling over the ringing of the bell buoy. The voice seemed to be saying, "I'm here right beside you to guide you." Then sleep came.

_____

Metronome: A triangular wooden instrument with metal pointer used to mark exact time.

Gunwales: The upper edges of the sides of a boat.

Fresnel Lens: Developed in France in 1822. This lens, with its multiple glass prisms, surrounded the lighthouse lamp. It had prisms at the top and bottom to reflect the light. A powerful magnifying glass in the middle concentrated the beam of light from the lamp. Weighted clockworks pumped kerosene from a reservoir to keep a jet lit and rotated the lens. Fresnel lenses were classified by order, the first order being the largest. The beacon from a 4th order Fresnel lens was visible for 12 miles out to sea.

Argand Lamp: Developed in England in 1812. This fountain lamp consisted of an oil (usually whale oil) reservoir, a burner with a hollow circular wick, and a lamp chimney. Each lamp had a parabolic reflector. A lighthouse might need up to forty of these lamps to provide an adequate beacon of light. Their wicks needed constant trimming and cleaning.

CHAPTER 6

First Day

Cock-a-doodle do!

Louie woke with a start. A beam of sunlight danced acrossthe room to the other bed. It was empty. His first thought was that Pa was in the lighthouse trimming the wicks and Ma was milking the cow in the shed. His job was to collect the eggs.

He threw off the quilt, stood up, and tried to get his bearings. Why was the room such a mess? Then he came to and remembered. This was Two Tree Island, not Swanton Point.

Everything that happened before today fast backwards to yesterday—to that fated day five months ago.

The storm that January had been particularly severe and lasted for days. Snow came in blinding sheets with hurricane force winds. It piled up in impossible drifts and roads were impassable. Louie and Ma helped Pa keep the lamp in the lighthouse lit day and night. They took turns winding the fog bell so that the bell rang every ten seconds. By the end of the fourth day they all were exhausted. Dampness permeated every corner of the lighthouse tower and even the house.

Louie and Ma were huddled around the coal stove trying to get warm and heat some coffee to take to Pa when they heard his call for help . . . and then a thud.

They both shouted "Coming" as they fought the wind and snow across the walkway to the entrance to the tower. When they reached the steps, they found Pa lying very still at the bottom. Ma screamed and tried to revive him, but it was no use.

They moved his body into the house and covered it. Ma cried. They both sat stunned by his lifeless body until morning when the winds died down and the snow stopped. Louie strapped on Pa's snow shoes and trudged through the snow drifts to town to get help. Ma stayed to keep the lamps lit and be with Pa's body.

The Lighthouse Board Superintendent arranged for Pa to be buried on Swanton Point in his lighthouse uniform. After that, Louie tried his best to keep up his studies and man the lighthouse the way Pa had taught him. Then the fear gripped him and the dream started. He couldn't concentrate on his school work and his grades fell. Even his best friend, Charlie, couldn't console him.

It took three months for the Lighthouse Board to send a new keeper. Louie and his mother showed the new keeper how to work the light and Louie helped her clean the house and pack their stuff. They moved to a boarding house in town until school ended. By then almost all their savings were gone.

Now it was the end of June and they were at a new lighthouse. Where did Ma go? It was too quiet. Louie's heart skipped a beat. He ran through the shed to the lighthouse steps. The hens flapped their wings as he passed them.

"Ma!"

"I'm extinguishing the lamp; be right down."

"Be careful!"

Panic pinched his brow. He almost stepped on an egg. But one of the hens let out a screech and he looked down and backed off. He picked up the egg gingerly and handed it to Ma. She fried it for their breakfast while Louie collected some water from the cisterns.

Next the two of them surveyed the house to see what needed to be done first.

"We'll start in the kitchen," Ma decided.

"Draw some water for washing."

Louie filled two buckets from the cisterns. By noon they had cleaned not only the kitchen but swept and dusted the other rooms on the first floor and settled all their supplies in proper places.

He climbed the stairs to the loft—just missing a broken step. Through one of two dormer windows he could see other islands in the distance. White sails dotted a sparkling green/blue sea. From the windows almost all of his new island home came into focus.

Rock ledges peeked out their ugly faces at various spots around the island. Rocks covered most of the land area except for where the lighthouse stood. Some field grass and bushes surrounded the house. Two evergreen trees at the other end of the island stood like prickly porcupines between an outcrop of rocks. A pipe from the outhouse led down into the water. Best not to swim there, thought Louie.

"Would you like to sleep in that loft?" Ma called from the bottom of the stairs.

"Wow! Would I ever!"

This would be his special place. He could carve his favorite birds and sea creatures with his new knife.

"We'll fix it up tomorrow but today we'll need to clean the shed and check the lamps and kerosene supply."

CHAPTER 7

Rainbow Arrives

L ouie's stomach growled.

"I'm starving, Ma. What's for dinner?"

"Guess we'll have to open some other cans," Ma replied, "but maybe after dinner you can catch us a fish for supper."

Louie had seen a fishing rod in the shed. It needed a line. No problem to string one with his new knife and fish hooks!

After an unappetizing but filling dinner of beans and brown bread, Louie grabbed the pole, put on his boots, took a bucket, and headed for a low spot on the island.

"Hope the fish are biting."

Low tide had exposed lots of seaweed covered rocks and even a small beach on the lee side of Two Tree Island. Louie filled his bucket with snails and a few mussels. He crushed them between some small rocks and urged the innards out with his fingers. He strung the fishing rod and tied on the fish hook. Then he stationed himself on the pier and waited for the fish to bite.

Discouraged after an hour without one bite, he looked up in surprise to see a tender tying up to a mooring. A man in a captain's hat lowered a launch from a davit. Louie heard the motor start and saw the boat head for the island.

"Ahoy, mate," shouted a figure at the helm. "Can you send down the cable? We've got some stuff for ye." The launch made a few slow circles, while Louie tried to start the motor for lowering the cable. Finally, he gave up and winched the cable down by hand. Quick as a jack rabbit, the man in the launch made fast the cable and came to Louie's aid. In no time the man had the engine working so that they could winch up the launch far above the cresting waves to unload its cargo.

"My name's Cap'n Bowline." He shook Louie's hand. "That there's the *Rainbow*." He pointed to the tender resting on the mooring.

"We tend buoys as well as haul supplies from the mainland when ye need 'em. Got yer flour and some other stuff in these boxes."

Captain Bowline handed the boxes over to Louie. By now Ma had seen the *Rainbow* and had come down the steps to greet their guest.

"Nice to meet ye, Mrs. Hollander. Missus and I thought you could use some fresh pollock and some of our home grown potatoes for your supper." He gave two bags to Louie's mother.

"Anything else ye need, I'll be return'n in a few days."

Louie's mother reminded him to bring their dairy cow. She gave him a list that she'd been making of other items she discovered they needed since yesterday.

"Well, I'll be on my way, then," said Captain Bowline. Louie winched the launch down into the sea and Captain Bowline loosened the cable.

"Oh, almost forgot the paint and brushes Mr. McAllister gave me to give to ye and these letters that came."

He started the motor and made a few circles, then headed back to the narrow pier.

Louie had to fend off the boat from the pier while transferring the remaining boxes and packages Captain Bowline passed up to him. Ma reached over just in time to grab the package of letters from his hand before they slid down into the foaming sea.

Louie helped Ma carry their new supplies up to the house as the *Rainbow* headed out to sea. Now he didn't need to keep fishing, at least until tomorrow.

Launch: Motorized boats, double-ender or dory, over 20 feet. They were often carried on davits on large tenders. Engines were make- or- break gasoline powered engines.

Davit: A crane on a ship that holds a lifeboat. It has gears that lower and hoist.

 Mooring: A buoy attached to a chain weighted down   with a concrete block to the bottom of the sea. A skipper can use a line from the chain to fasten a boat without using an anchor.

Lee side: Side away from the prevailing wind.

CHAPTER 8

Lighthouse Keeping

O ne of these letters is for you, Louie." Ma said.

"It's from Charlie!" Louie exclaimed, tearing open the envelope. He read and reread it.

He put the letter aside. Keeping took up the rest of the day. Louie cleaned out the shed. He found a hammer and some nails in a can and collected all the loose coal and put it back into the bin. His overalls were covered with coal dust when he finished. He checked the kerosene level in the oil shed. There seemed to be enough to last though the summer. He repaired the roost for the hens and placed a box underneath with some packing straw to catch the eggs. He even found an old barrel for feed storage in one of the other sheds.

Before supper Louie had to change into a pair of his too-short knickers. He hated them, but Ma had to wash his overalls and hang them on the line outside to dry.

He followed Ma up the lighthouse stairs with a can of kerosene to fill the lamp reservoir and light the lamp jet. Louie took the polishing cloth and cleaned each prism until it sparkled. He wound up the clockwork mechanism that rotated the beacon and even remembered to empty the brass dust pan.

While his mother lit the jet, Louie explored the lighthouse tower one more time. He found an old chart hanging on the wall next to a log book.

"Hey, Ma. We forgot to write in the log yesterday."

Ma took the log book and wrote:

Thursday, June 25, 1903. *Landed at six P.M. Wind 15 SW. Fair. Cleaned lighthouse and lit lamp.*
Friday, June 26, 1903. *Cleaned house and shed.* Wind *10 W. Rainbow brought supplies. Clear.*

Molly Hollander with son Louie.

"How would you like to keep the log during the day for the rest of the month, Louie, now that you're the man of the family? You write in the log book when it's time to rotate the lens. You can do that, too."

Louie puffed out his chest and pocketed the pen. In spite of the knickers he felt more like a man tonight. He couldn't wait to name and memorize all the islands on the chart.

Louie spotted a list of *Instructions to Light-Keepers* posted inside the tower. Louie read them out loud:

"The utmost neatness of buildings and premises is demanded. Bedrooms, as well as other parts of the dwelling, must be neatly kept. Untidiness will be strongly reprehended, and its continuance will subject a keeper to dismissal. The premises must be kept clean and well whitewashed; grounds in order; all the inside painted work of the lanterns well washed, and, when required retouched with paint. The spare articles embraced in the list of allowances must be kept on hand and examined frequently, and should be kept clean and in order for use."[1]

"I guess the former keeper hadn't looked at these for awhile," Ma chuckled.

They ate fish chowder Louie's mother prepared from the pollock fish, potatoes, and canned milk with hard sea biscuits for supper. Then she listened as Louie read a Bible passage—another tradition he had taken over from his father.

Before the last of their evening prayers that night, Louie fell asleep. The wind whistled softly, the waves lapped against the rocks, and a beam of warm light careened across his bed. He dreamed that he and Charlie were playing baseball at Swanton Point.

---

[1] Mary Louise Clifford and Candace Clifford, *Women Who Kept the Lghts*, Cypress Communications. 1993. 124.

CHAPTER 9

Lighthouse Chores

A busy day followed.

"We'll need some wood to fire the stove," his mother announced at breakfast, "so after your morning chores you can go around the island and bring back any driftwood you find lying around."

Morning chores constituted first collecting the eggs the hens had laid the night before, after the wake up call by the rooster; next, raising the American flag; then, fishing. Louie baited the hook and waited for a fish to bite while his mother extinguished the lamp and cooked their breakfast. After breakfast he wrote in the lighthouse log.

Louie found some driftwood and old planks. He piled them beside one of the sheds. One special piece of driftwood caught his attention. Imagining a few birds he could carve in it, he set it aside till he had his room ready. The planks would do for repairing the step to the loft. He'd bring the axe back later and chop up the other pieces for starting fires.

Gathering the wood gave him an opportunity to explore the perimeter of his new island home. The side of the island away from the entrance to the harbor gradually slopped down to the water's edge. This gave Louie an idea.

I might build a better boat ramp here, he thought, better than climbing down those steps on the other side and lugging the double-ender to the tramway and winching it down.

At Swanton Point he had built birdhouses and helped his Pa build a new pier. They even had a float, until it had blown apart in a storm, the same storm that blew Grandpa into the raging sea.

Grandpa had been staying with them that winter, helping with the lighthouse chores and building the float. He slipped on an icy patch on the walkway. The wind had blown apart the railing so that he slid right through into the raging ocean. Before Pa could reach him, the waves dashed his body against the rocks. That happened two years before his Pa's death. Louie missed them both.

After dinner, Louie sawed one of the planks to replace the broken one on the stairs to the loft and nailed it into place. With Ma's help, Louie dusted and cleaned his new room. There were several cots, a table and chair, an armoire, and a bookcase. They moved up one of the beds from the downstairs bedroom and folded up the cots that occupied the rest of the space.

Before they realized it the sun had begun to set.

"Supper will have to wait until after we've taken care of the beacon and written in the log."

Louie scattered seed for the hens and rooster on his way to the Lighthouse tower.

My first log entry, thought Louie as he entered that day's happenings.

June 27, 1903. *Cleaned and tended house and tower.*
Wind SE. 10. Fair.

Louie Hollander

Armoire: Free standing tall cupboard or wardrobe.

CHAPTER 10

Fog in

A fog mull.

Ma stopped kneading the bread dough when she looked out the window the next morning and saw it coming in.

"Where's the fog horn?" Ma said. "Have you seen it, Louie?"

"Think I saw it in one of those other sheds."

"Better find it and see if we can get it to work and be ready to light that lamp. Fog could roll in any time."

She left the bread to rise and grabbed the kerosene can. Louie went to look in the remaining sheds. He found the fog horn in a shed behind the house.

Contraption was more like it, Louie thought. It had pulleys all over and around it were assorted other bits of machinery. He'd never seen one before. On Swanton Point they'd only had a bell. He'd seen a bell hanging on the cone shaped shed at the base of the lighthouse tower.

"Can't figure out how to work this machine. Can't find instructions," he told Ma.

"Run up to the tower and see if there are any there. Mr. McAllister and the keeper certainly didn't give us any."

Louie took the tower steps two by two. 2,4,6,8 . . . He counted forty-eight stairs and had to stop to breathe on the landing halfway up. He looked all around the Fresnel lens and on the stand with the log book and chart but couldn't find any instructions except for those about keeping the lighthouse clean. The fog bank was closing in.

"Quick Ma," he called down the stairs. "We better get the lamp lit. I'll ring the bell until we can figure out how to work that fog horn engine. Lots of boats out there today."

Louie polished the lenses while his mother filled the reservoir with kerosene and lit the lamp. Louie wound up the clockwork so that the beacon could rotate its beam of white light to all passing ships.

By this time fog had surrounded the tower. Louie went outside to ring the bell—every ten seconds. His mother brought him his oil skin jacket and some crackers with a piece of fish left over from breakfast. They took turns ringing the bell the rest of the afternoon through the evening—one hour on and one hour off—while the other one tried to figure out how to start the fog horn machine. They cleaned the lamp jet, rewound the clockwork, and refilled the reservoir and gave up on the fog horn shortly before midnight.

After twelve hours of on-and-off vigil Louie was bone tired. Every time he rang the bell his body vibrated. He thought he heard his Pa cry for help and then the familiar thud. He shivered. The swirling fog began to look like his Pa's head with a trailing plume.

"Look Louie," his mother tapped him on the shoulder, "you can see some stars and I think the wind has shifted. The fog will lift soon."

Sure enough by morning the fog had lifted and a stiff wind was blowing. The barometer pointed to *FAIR*.

Neither one of them had slept much because of tending the lamps and the bell during the night. So when the rooster crowed they extinguished the lamp and slept for a few hours.

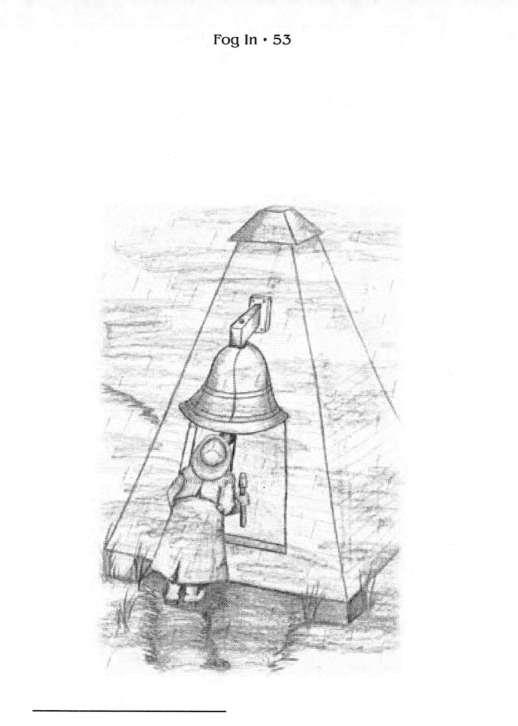

Fog Mull: A bank or cloud of condensed water vapor close to the ground that obliterates objects.

CHAPTER 11

Company

Voices downstairs woke Louie up.

Who could his mother be talking to? He wondered. He dressed quickly and started down the loft steps. Halfway down he saw three men. Seated in the parlor were Mr. McAllister, a man with a white collar, and one man dressed in overalls.

"Please meet the visiting preacher, Reverend Sam Hornblower," Mr. McAllister was saying to Ma. He turned when he heard Louie come down the steps.

"Morning, son, hear you had a rough night. Forgot to tell you that we were installing a new fog horn in that shed back there."

Mr. McAllister pointed toward the direction of the shed where Louie had seen the fog horn the day before.

Next, he introduced Louie and Ma to the machinist, Harry.

"Harry will be installing and showing you how to work the horn. Reverend and I will stay around. After your Ma fixes us some victuals we will have a rip, roaring Sunday worship—only on Monday."

Louie's jaw dropped. He needed more sleep—not have Mr. McAllister around!

"Got to tend the hens ." He made a bee line for the shed.

"Oh . . . Captain Bowline will be bringing back your milk cow in the tender when he comes to fetch us!" he shouted after Louie.

Louie took his time in the work shed. He followed Harry to the new shed where the fog horn sat. He watched while Harry installed the new machine.

By the time Louie arrived back at the house, Mr. McAllister and Reverend Hornblower were sitting down at the kitchen table and Ma, in her best skirt and apron, was serving them oatmeal, fresh bread, and eggs.

"Your Ma told me about your pa." Reverend Hornblower got up and gave Louie his chair.

"You must really miss him."

"Yeh," Louie responded as he spooned his oatmeal and grabbed a piece of bread. He wondered if this man knew about his dream, too.

After breakfast Louie changed into his lighthouse jacket. The group gathered to begin worshiping with a hymn-sing. Next, Reverend Hornblower read the story from the Bible about Jesus appearing to his disciples while they were cooking fish on the beach after he had been crucified. Then they talked about it.

"Boy, they must have been surprised to see him when they thought he was dead," Louie commented. "I thought I saw my Pa last night in the fog and sometimes I hear his voice."

Reverend Hornblower nodded. He explained that Jesus is always with us, especially when we get discouraged and things go bad. He gave Louie some Sunday school papers and asked if Louie would show him around the island.

Louie jumped up.

"Sure."

Anything to get away from Mr. McAllister. He couldn't stand to be called "son" or "boy" one more time. But he didn't dare tell him so. Maybe he could tell this preacher though.

Louie took Reverend Hornblower first up to the tower to examine the Fresnel lens and look at the view of the bay. Next, he took him to the low place on the island.

"Here's where I want to build a better boat ramp. When we lived on Swanton Point I helped my Pa build a new pier. Now it's just me and Ma."

"I lost my dad when I was about your age," Reverend Hornblower said, "he was a member of the Life Saving Service. He died during a storm like your pa. He was trying to rescue a floundering sloop. He left me on the shore and I had to watch his dory capsize. I dreamt I saw him drowning and couldn't rescue him for months afterward. I thought it was my fault he had drowned."

"Gee," Louie replied, "I have dreams, too."

He told the preacher about his dream and the voice.

"Maybe that's Jesus voice," Reverend Hornblower said, "coming to tell you he's there beside you just as he did his disciples when they were lonely and sad."

An hour later Mr. McAllister found them still sitting and talking.

"Harry's ready to show Mrs. Hollander how to work the fog horn. Bring Louie and come and join us," he said to Reverend Hornblower. They all gathered round the fog horn machine while Harry showed them how to generate a head of steam until it could make a moaning sound through its diaphone horn.

"You'll need these directions to keep the horn in working order." Harry handed Ma a pamphlet. Then, he let both of them try cranking up the engine.

"Sure beats ringing that bell," Ma said. "It'll make foggy day lighthouse tending easier."

Ma fixed them corned beef hash, sea biscuits with canned peaches for dinner.

By mid afternoon, the *Rainbow* had arrived back to its mooring.

"Got your cow aboard. Need help gett'n her hoisted up and down into the launch, then holding her steady," shouted Captain Bowline from the launch.

Louie's mother clapped her hands. "Now we can have fresh milk and butter!"

Harry and Reverend Hornblower each managed to jump into the launch from the pier on a cresting wave.

Louie, Ma, and Mr. McAllister watched from shore while the three men hoisted the mooing cow up with a sling and then down into the launch. They could see the cow struggling against the ropes holding her in place while the launch made its slow way back to the waiting tramway. Louie started the motor to lower the cable for Harry to grab it.

"She darn near upset the launch," moaned Captain Bowline. "She 'mooed' all the way over and dropped dung, too."

It took all of them to lift the cow with the ropes out of the launch once the boat had been winched up the tramway. Captain Bowline motored the launch back to the tender to collect a bale of straw while Ma coaxed and Louie and Harry pushed the reluctant cow up the steep rock steps. It took them an hour before the cow was safely installed in her new shed.

"Goodbye, son," called Mr. McAllister as the launch motored away for the last time.

"My name's Louie," Louie called back.

He felt like a ton of bricks had been lifted off his chest. Reverend Hornblower even promised to return and take him fishing in their double-ender.

What a great day, he thought.

That night he wrote:

June 29, 1903: Wind NE 10. Clear. Officer McAllister and crew in-stalled mechanical fog horn. Visiting preacher: Rev. Hornblower.

Louie Hollander

Diaphone: A fog signal similar to a siren but producing a blast of two tones.

CHAPTER 12

Fishing Buddies

With the new fog horn working, Louie had more time to roam the island or read his magazines and books.

Reading *Tom Sawyer*'s adventures on the Mississippi River took him far away from the intermittent fog and the confines of his island home. He missed the community clambake and fireworks in town on the 4th of July because the fog was in that day so he had to help tend the light and horn.

Betsy, their new cow, gave them plenty of milk and Louie loved churning the butter for their biscuits and bread that his mother made every day.

On the first sunny day, Louie turned over a small plot of earth around the bushes for his mother to plant beet, radish, and carrot seeds as well as some beans and lettuce.

"Hope we're not too late in the growing season," she said as she scattered the seed in the trenches Louie had made.

"All we need is some rain."

"Not much water left in the cisterns, either" Louie cautioned.

"We'll have to conserve then," his mother replied, "and pray for rain. Maybe Captain Bowline can fetch us some fresh water from the mainland."

"And I'll bring seawater to boil for washing and for bathing," Louie added.

At supper, Ma announced: "How would you like Charlie to come to stay with us for the month of August?" Louie nearly upset his chair. He missed his best school friend. Charlie had written about playing baseball and going fishing in the *Tipsy*, his pa's fishing schooner.

"Can he?" asked Louie.

"I think it would be a great idea," his mother replied. "Besides, we could use an extra hand helping with the light, painting, and building that boat ramp you want to build. I'll write his mother and father tonight and we can send it with Captain Bowline when he comes tomorrow."

After supper, Louie wrote a letter to Charlie. His mother wrote one to Charlie's parents.

"God, please let him come," Louie prayed that night, "and don't forget the rain."

When the *Rainbow* arrived the next day, Louie ran down the rock steps to greet Captain Bowline waving the two letters. To his surprise, Reverend Hornblower waved back.

"Ready for some serious fishing, Louie?" he called.

Louie beamed. He had no time to take the double-ender out yet, nor could he carry it to the wharf by himself. They walked back up to the house together.

"Be back after I make my rounds to fetch ye," called Captain Bowline as he headed out to check the buoys.

"Could you spare this young man for a few hours, Mrs. Hollander?" Reverend Hornblower asked.

"We have some serious fishing and rowing to do."

Louie's mother grinned. "Take that young man away. He's getting on my nerves."

"And if we're going to be fishing buddies no more calling me Reverend. 'Uncle' Sam will do."

Louie lost no time in collecting his fishing rod and bait. Uncle Sam had his pole and fancy worms for bait.

Launching the double-ender proved to be a daunting task. Each took an end. By lifting and carrying the boat across the rock face they finally managed to line it up in position on the tramway. Then, they fastened the cable to the bow. Uncle Sam helped Louie start the motor on the winch.

"Who's going to be the first to row?" asked Uncle Sam after they were both in the boat.

"Can I?" asked Louie.

"Does he know how?" Uncle Sam turned to Ma.

"Learned to row when he was eight," she answered.

"Ok, Louie. Oars up. Ready?"

They steadied themselves in their places in the boat as Ma lowered the cable.

As soon as the boat landed in the water, Louie rowed her expertly away from the island.

"Let's go near those lobster buoys." Uncle Sam pointed. "Fish usually gather there."

They spent the next two hours rowing, fishing, and talking.

Uncle Sam reported on the latest baseball news. "Wireless reports Boston Pilgrims are on a winning streak."

"How's Cy Jones average . . .?" Louie's line tightened.

"I've got a bite." The line slackened.

"Must have got away."

Just when they were ready to row for home, Louie had a big bite. His pole bent as the fish struggled to get free. With Uncle Sam's help he landed a seven inch flounder.

They unhooked the fish and let him thrash around in the bottom of the boat. Louie suggested Uncle Sam take his turn rowing and go around to the other side of the island to the beach where he had collected bait at low tide. Since the tide had ebbed, they found the beach and were able to land the boat and pull her up. They tied the painter around a higher rock above the seaweed.

Louie proudly showed his fish to Ma who had come down to the shore to greet them. Uncle Sam helped Louie clean the flounder. Ma cooked it and they ate it with blueberry muffins she had just made. After dinner, when the tide had begun to flow, they carried the double-ender to its shed.

Louie told Uncle Sam about inviting Charlie and gave him their letters to post.

"I'll take them to the post office myself as soon as I get back to town," Uncle Sam promised as the *Rainbow* pulled away for its return voyage.

"And don't forget to bring us some fresh water," Louie's mother called.

Louie waved. He hated to see his fishing buddy leave.

Cistern: Tanks for collecting rain water on island lighthouses. They were made of metal or cement. Rain water was collected off roofs and channeled through gutters and downspouts through pipes to underground tanks.

Lobster Buoys: Wooden shaped markers tied to a rope leading to an underground trap to catch lobsters. Each lobster man designs his own buoys with distinct colors and markings.

CHAPTER 13

Jonah Lesson

The *Rainbow* launch returned on Monday carrying three passengers—Uncle Sam, a woman dressed in a bonnet, and next to her, a boy.

"Thought ye'd like to meet the missus," said Captain Bowline, "Name's Penny, and my son, Tommy. He's about eight. Thought we'd join ye for Monday worship if ye don't mind."

After the *Rainbow* had been winched up the tramway and secured, Penny handed Ma a basket.

"Pleased to meet ye. Thought ye'd like some fresh veg'tables. Imagine ye haven't had time to grow 'em yet," Penny said.

Louie's mother thanked her, took the basket, and then helped Penny over the gunwales of the boat.

Captain Bowline handed Louie two jugs.

"Here's some jugs of fresh water, too, to tide you over. From the looks of the clouds though expect ye'll refill those cisterns tomorrow."

Uncle Sam followed Captain Bowline up the steps to the house. When they were settled in the parlor, worshiping began with a hymn-sing. Then Uncle Sam asked the captain to read the Bible passage about Jonah and the big fish.

Louie wondered what it would be like to be inside the belly of a fish.

"Pretty dark inside that fish," Reverend Hornblower began.

"Jonah tried to run away from what God wanted him to do and he had to stay in that darkness for three days until he said, 'Ok God, it's your show, not mine. I'll go to Nineveh.' Even when he got to Nineveh and delivered God's message Jonah still didn't want God's message to come true. So he sat down under a tree and sulked.

How many of us don't want to do what we ought to be doing or want something that we cannot have?"

All heads nodded. Louie thought about the new clothes his mother had promised, but hadn't gotten.

After dinner, Louie took Tommy around the island, holding his hand tight. Since the tide had ebbed, they found some hermit crabs on the beach. They stepped on seaweed bladders and made up a song that went like this, "Snap-pop; hop-pop; stop." They took off their shoes and socks and waded in a salt water pool left by the receding sea. They collected some driftwood and built a fort.

All too soon, they heard, "Board'n time!" from Captain Bowline.

When they were ready to get back in the launch, Penny Bowline turned to Ma.

"We'd like ye to come to the town clam bake next Sunday."

"Who will tend the light?" Ma asked.

"I'll clear it with Mr. McAllister so's he can send a relief man for a few hours," Captain Bowline assured her. He agreed to take them in his launch to the clambake and return them home later that afternoon.

"Depending on the weather, of course."

Louie knew what that meant. The whims of the weather fixed the limits for any long range planning. Louie had learned to live with those whims. In foggy and stormy weather, seamen's lives depended on them keeping the lamp lit and the fog horn working on Two Tree Island.

Seaweed bladders: Air pockets in seaweed that keep seaweed floating upright under water, like a balloon. Seaweed are large algae plants that grow in salt water and produce their own photosynthesis. Certain seaweeds can be eaten. They're often used for fertilizer or in medicines.

CHAPTER 14

Lighthouse Pet

The barometer read *CHANGE*.

Louie noted it in the log book that evening. Sure enough, Captain Bowline's predictions came true. When Louie awoke the next morning, he heard the rain hitting the window panes.

"We're in for a three day Nor' Eastern," Ma announced after breakfast.

"Wind shifted during the night. We'll have to keep the lamp lit all day and maybe start the fog horn if the visibility gets bad."

By noon thick fog accompanied the rain. Louie and Ma took turns cleaning the lamp, emptying the brass dust pan, keeping the reservoir filled with kerosene, and the beacon rotating. Periodically, they had to wipe off the soot from the lens; also, keep the coal fire lit for the steam engine to work for the fog horn. The latter proved a formidable task in damp weather!

Louie prayed that their new horn would not break down—as he heard many of them did. Harry had left some spare rubber rings and other parts. But Louie wasn't sure he could fix anything that broke and he really didn't want to have to stand outside to crank the bell clapper every four hours.

In between shifts in the lighthouse tower, Louie or Ma stocked the stove with coal to keep the inside of the house warm. They put on their boots and oilskin jackets when they had to go outside. Louie offered to milk Betsy and feed the hens and rooster, who really didn't like being out in the rain and getting their feathers wet. Betsy just wanted to lie down. The hens buried their heads in their feathers and stayed on their roost. Louie wanted to lie down, too. When he did crawl under the quilt just to get warm, he couldn't fall asleep. He had to keep his ears tuned to the sound of the fog horn and his eyes focused to the sweep of the beacon of light from the tower.

By the second day of the storm, Louie and Ma moved like zombies. In the back of Louie's mind, he remembered his Pa's fall at the end of that bad storm on Swanton Point.

"Hey, Ma." He took her arm that night while they were huddled around the stove. She looked as tired as he felt.

"I don't want either of us falling like Pa did or something worse. How can we each get some sleep?"

"No use both of us worrying about the light and horn," replied Ma.

"I'll get some cotton for our ears and we'll tie a dark piece of cloth around our eyes when we lie down. We'll do four hour shifts. One to tend and one to sleep. If anything happens we'll agree to wake the other one up."

Both were able to get some much needed sleep with this new scheme. By the end of the third day the rain had lightened and the fog began to lift. But the fog horn stuttered and stopped so they had to winch the fog bell. Even that broke down so Louie had to ring the bell by hand.

His arms ached and he shivered in the dampness. Even with a heavy sweater under his oilskin jacket he felt chilled.

"Kuk! Kuk! Kuk!" Louie heard a seagull call close by. He looked up just as the seagull was about to fly into the tower glass window above him.

"Shoo! Fly away!" he warned the seagull.

So many birds had died flying into the lighthouse tower at Swanton Point. Louie had picked up each one that had crashed. Some were just stunned and in time were able to get their bearings and fly away. Others were too badly broken and died. Louie often held them and stroked them before they died, then buried them in a seaweed grave. They became models for his wood carvings.

"Shoo!" he called to the seagull again but it was too late. The seagull hit the glass with a thud and fell, landing beside Louie. Louie picked him up. The bird heaved and gasped for breath.

"Calm down."

Louie stroked the brown gull's wet feathers. The gull flapped one wing but the other lay still beside his body. Must have broken his wing, Louie thought. He held the gull in his lap until his mother tapped him on the shoulder.

"Let's try one more time to get this fog bell clapper winch started."

Together they winched. After several tries, with both of their weights, they got the winch to work.

"I'm going to take this young Herring gull inside to get warm," Louie told Ma, "seems he has broken his wing."

Louie took the damaged gull inside and taped his broken wing. He put some fish with bread and milk in a dish and tried to encourage the gull to drink and eat. But the gull just looked up and squinted his eyes.

The next day dawned bright and clear. Louie made a nest for the gull in a box by his bed. The gull drank some milk and ate some fish bits and bread with Louie's stroking and coaxing. He especially liked to eat the food from Louie's dish. Louie named him Sammy, after his friend, Uncle Sam.

Sammy followed Louie around while Louie did his chores, except when he tended the hens. The rooster made a big fuss whenever Sammy came near so that Sammy learned to stay away.

Sammy perched on a rock near Louie while Louie milked the cow and walked beside him when Louie went down to the pier to fish every day. Louie carried Sammy with him when he went up the lighthouse steps to tend the lights and let him perch on the railing around the catwalk.

"Someday you'll be able to fly again," he said to the gull.

Sammy liked to perch on Louie's shoulder and watch him write in the log book. Sometimes he sat on the winch handle while Louie wound the clock mechanism to rotate the light beacon. He could only be diverted by food placed by Louie on the catwalk around the tower.

"When he's well enough, he will fly away," his mother noted.

Sometimes Sammy flapped his good wing but his mending wing just fluttered at his side. When Louie decided to fix and start to paint the broken shutters, he added a few green spots to Sammy's brown coat.

Catwalk: A narrow walkway at the top of a lighthouse tower surrounding the lighthouse lenses and windows.

Herring Gull: The most popular seagull along the coast line. Young
herring gulls are light brown in color, sometimes with spots. They
grow to be white bodied with a gray back, black wing tips, and a
yellow beak. They can be as long as 11–31 inches. They are scav-
enger birds but like fish and shell fish the best.

CHAPTER 15

Clam Bake

A hoy, mate!" Captain Bowline called the following Sunday afternoon.

The weather dawned fair and clear, clear enough for Captain Bowline to bring his launch to pick up Louie and Ma to town for the Sunday clambake.

Louie had debated what to wear. He didn't want to wear his too-tight-and-short trousers or his knickers.

"Ma, I'll really look dumb around the other kids," he begged and whined. Ma just ignored his complaints. He finally put on the knickers when he heard Captain Bowline's shout.

After Louie had winched up the launch, Ma came down the steps carrying something over her arm.

"Thought you might rather wear these instead of those knickers you hate." She handed Louie some trousers.

"They're your pa's. I shortened them and took in the seams. Think they'll fit you now." She smiled.

Louie grabbed the trousers and went back up to the house to try them on. They fit perfectly! Now he could face the other kids at the picnic.

"Aussie!" exclaimed Ma when she saw another man getting out of the launch.

"Got recruited as relief keeper." Aussie helped Ma into the boat.

"Enjoy yerselves," he called as he winched down the launch and waved goodbye.

Children were climbing all over rocks by the shore when Louie arrived. Men were cooking lobsters, clams, corn, and potatoes over a big fire. Women were setting up the other food on picnic tables.

At first Louie felt awkward and confused with so many folks around, even wearing his new trousers. Penny Bowline took Ma over to meet the other adults while Louie just stood, looking at the ground and shuffling his feet.

Tommy came running up and grabbed Louie's hand. He dragged him down to the shore where some of the other children were playing.

"This here's Louie," Tommy announced, "he lives on Two Tree Island."

The other children gathered around Louie and asked him all kinds of questions about Two Tree Island.

"Is it boring on that island?"

"Who do you play with?"

"Do you have any pets?"

"Do you help tend the lighthouse?"

"What makes the light work?"

Louie told them all about Sammy, his pet gull, and showed them one of the bird carvings he had made. His feelings of awkwardness began to disappear.

Louie and Ma could only stay for four hours. Lighthouse Board regulations specified only six hours away from the lighthouse during the day and it took an hour to get back to Two Tree Island.

The next day the *Rainbow* brought Harry, the machinist, to repair the fog horn. While he worked Captain Bowline helped Louie move some wooden planks that had washed up on shore in the storm to the site for the proposed boat ramp.

"How do you propose to hold these in place?" he asked Louie.

"Well . . ., we could cement them to the rocks."

"Sounds like you've thought this one through" replied Captain Bowline. "I'll bring the cement and mix it next time I come."

Louie missed his pa less and less since Uncle Sam and Captain Bowline had agreed to help him build the new boat ramp. Now Louie still had to depend on Uncle Sam to help him move their dory to the tramway to take him fishing. Meanwhile Sammy kept him company when Louie fished from the pier.

"That's Red buoy #four, Black buoy #three, and Spindle Bell." Louie wrote these names on the chart when Captain Bowline pointed them out.

"*Moonbeam*, *Lady Luck*, *Enterprise*, and *Spanish Main*." Louie pointed to the names he had written down in the log book of the, steamers, sloops, and schooners that frequently passed Two Tree Island.

"The *Spanish Main* passes by the most." Louie noted the number of times he had written her name in the log book. "I think she must be bringing sardines into the plant over at Wishing Cove."

Louie liked to watch the sailing sloops and schooners. He wondered what it would be like to sail in one of them.

Buoys and Bells and Spars: Mark rock ledges and channels to help ships navigate safely.

Schooner: A fore and aft rigged large sailing vessel with two masts and many sails. These sailing ships were used for fishing and carried dories for setting out trawl lines with hundreds of hooks for bottom fish. They were used for fishing on offshore banks along the east coast before trawlers.

Sloop: A sailing vessel with one mast and at least two sails. Sloops were popular fishing vessels in early 1900s.

CHAPTER 16

Inspection

I t couldn't be! He's not due yet!"

While fishing from the pier one morning, Louie saw a tender flying a lighthouse flag approaching. Sheilding his eyes from the glare of the morning sun, he looked again.

"Ha! Ha! Ha!" Sammy responded as the tender drew closer. Sammy had perched on his special spot on a piling watching Louie fish.

Even though Mr. McAllister had told them during the interview that the Lighthouse Board Inspector would come around every three months, Louie knew Ma was not ready for him so soon.

Several foggy days and repairing the fog horn had delayed the necessary painting needing to be finished in order to meet lighthouse inspection regulations. Ma hadn't done much cleaning to the house since that first week. They'd even relaxed from keeping the Fresnel lens and lighthouse tower windows soot free.

"More important to get settled and make new friends," Ma had conceded to Penny Bowline at the clam bake.

Louie dropped his fishing rod and ran up the steps to alert Ma. Sammy's hop was more like a jump-glide as he flapped his good wing to keep up with Louie. He fell on his beak once.

Louie picked him up and carried him under his arm.

"He's here!" he shouted.

"Who?" His mother came to the door wiping her apron.

"The Lighthouse Board . . ." he stopped to catch his breath. ". . . the inspector!"

"Quick, Louie, climb up to the lighthouse tower and make sure the dust pan has been emptied. I'll tidy up the house best I can and put on my uniform."

Louie put Sammy down and ran through the shed to the tower. Sammy ran after him squawking. The rooster scolded and the hens scattered. Louie took the tower steps two by two leaving Sammy at the bottom to "Kuk! Kuk!" at him for being left behind.

Louie emptied the brass dust pan into the black coal bucket. He almost tripped as he ran back down the steps. Then, he left the pan and bucket and ran down the hill to winch down the cable hand over hand just as the tender's dory reached the bottom of the ramp. Meanwhile Louie scrambled to start the motor to haul up the boat. An inspector in his blue jacket with the lighthouse shield on his hat stepped out looking very official.

Louie saluted him and the inspector saluted back.

"I have come to see Molly Hollander and to inspect the lighthouse."

"I'll fetch her," Louie said as he walked the men slowly up the winding steps to the house. He wanted to give his mother enough time to clean up the house. Meanwhile Sammy caught up and walked silently behind Louie, trying to keep step.

Louie's mother came to the door. She had at least had time to remove her apron and put on her blue jacket with the brass buttons. His jacket still hung in his armoire. She greeted the two men as she pushed a loose lock of hair under her lighthouse cap.

"Morning, Mrs. Hollander. I'm here for this month's inspection. Name's Cleveland. First I wish to check the light house tower," he said as he pulled on his white inspection gloves.

At that moment, Louie remembered he had forgotten to take a rag and wipe the dust pan after he had emptied it. Hope he doesn't check that, he thought as he followed his mother and Cleveland up the lighthouse tower steps.

"I want to see your dust pan," Cleveland demanded. Louie felt like hiding.

"Dirty," said the inspector disgustedly as he ran his finger over the dustpan. He made a large black X in his notebook beside the line for "brass dust pan." Then, he ran his fingers around the lamp

lens, and, finally, over the windows in the tower to be sure they were all soot free. He checked to see if the clock mechanism operated to rotate the lens.

"Okay here," he nodded as he put small checkmarks beside lamp lens, windows, and clockwork mechanism.

How did she do it? Louie thought. Ma must have wiped the lens and windows early this morning while he was fishing.

"Looks like the brass needs some polishing," Cleveland said. Another big X went beside "brass polished." Louie sighed. That was his chore and he hadn't gotten around to it.

Cleveland checked the supply of kerosene and inspected the fog horn machine.

Next he walked around the house. "Shutters need painting and whitewash in bad shape." Another big X went beside "outside upkeep."

"Now I need to inspect the house," he told Ma.

"Please come in." Ma ushered Cleveland into the parlor. "We've tried to clean up after the last keeper. But it's taken longer than we thought."

Louie hoped he'd accept her reasoning. Besides, didn't he know they had just lost Pa six months ago! Resentment gnawed at his innards and he clenched and unclenched his hands.

First, Cleveland inspected the kitchen. He wrote down "cobweb in corner" besides "kitchen" with another big X. He put a check beside kitchen stove. At least he didn't wipe his gloves on that, thought Louie.

Louie's mother invited Cleveland to sit down in the parlor. He pocketed his white gloves and unbuttoned his jacket. She served him a cup of coffee and some biscuits she had made.

"Good biscuits, Ma'am," he said. "Best I've tasted from all the lighthouses I've visited."

When he had finished his coffee and biscuits, he climbed up to the loft. He glanced around the room and looked out the dormer windows. Louie's clothes lay scattered around the room along with his magazines and wood carvings. Another big X, Louie thought.

"Well, Ma'am," Cleveland said, after he had returned from his tour of the other bedrooms, "you've done a right fine job for such a short time being here. The light and fog horn are in working order. Your report will be satisfactory except for that dirty dust pan in the tower, some brass polishing needing to be done, some painting for the exterior, and some dusting needed on the interior.

Son . . ." Louie froze and looked at the ground, "next time we come we expect you to be in uniform." Louie felt a lump in the pit of his stomach.

"Yes, Sir!" Louie stood at attention and saluted.

"We've brought you another tank of kerosene."

He beckoned to the seamen below. The seamen, who had taken the launch out to the tender during the inspection, stood at attention by a tank and a smaller chest.

"If you have any more problems with your fog horn, tell Captain Bowline. He'll bring the machinist as soon as he has some spare time."

"We brought you a Lighthouse Service medicine chest, too—standard equipment: iodine, tooth pullers, quinine pills, castor oil, sweet spirits of niter, morphine, and camphor pills. Anything else you need, visiting nurse will come round with the *Rainbow*. In an emergency, raise the SOS flag in the trunk for extra help."

The seamen replaced the old kerosene tank with the new one and brought Ma the medicine chest. They all got back in their launch and waited for the wave to crest so Louie could lower it into the sea.

"My name is Louie," Louie called softly to their backs as they motored away. "Louie, Louie, Louie," the wind picked up the name and carried it out to sea.

CHAPTER 17

Waiting

Charlie could arrive any day.

July rushed toward August as Louie crossed off the days on the calender on the wall. July 8, 9, 10 . . . 23, 24, 25 . . ."

Charlie's parents had replied to Ma's invitation saying that they would bring Charlie down in their fishing schooner, *Tipsy*, toward the end of the month. He could stay until school started in September.

Louie spent more time in the lighthouse tower, Sammy by his side, scanning the ships to see if he could see Charlie's pa's schooner. He wished he had a spy glass. Charlie often took him up to the widow's walk at the top of his house to look for the *Tipsy* returning from a fishing trip. However, without a spy glass all the schooners looked alike.

Moonbeam and *Spanish Main* but no *Tipsy* came by Two Tree Island.

Every time the *Rainbow* arrived bringing supplies or Uncle Sam, Captain Bowline shook his head.

"Like enough, she'll be appearing one of these days. Soon's I see her, I'll lead her to this island. Don't go fretting now, lad."

"By the by, here's the cement ye be wanting." Captain Bowline handed Louie a bag of cement. Uncle Sam helped Louie mix it and cement down the wooden planks just at the right places on the rock surface. But they needed more planks before they could finish. Captain Bowline offered to search for flotsam containing wooden planks as well as a fishing schooner named Tipsy.

Meanwhile, Louie tried to coax Sammy to use his healed wing. Whenever Sammy followed him around, Louie turned, looked at him, and flapped his arms.

"Fly, Sammy–this way."

"Try it Sammy, don't be scared."

He tried to persuade Sammy to fly off the railing on the catwalk around the lighthouse tower. But Sammy would look at Louie, cock his head and say, "Kuk?"

"See other gulls are flying. Don't you want to join them?" Louie pointed to other gulls flying around the island. Sammy just stood and squinted his eyes at Louie.

Finally, when Louie had checked off all the July days on his wall calender, the Tipsy appeared over the horizon.

Flotsam: Floating debris or wreckage from a sunken ship.

Chapter 18

Temptation

M a, he's here!" Louie shouted from the lighthouse tower when he saw the familiar schooner.

Louie almost tripped over Sammy as he hurried down the steps to start the winch engine.

The *Tipsy*'s dory headed for the ramp. Charlie's father said, "Ayuh" as he reached over to grab the cable handing it over to a tall boy in the bow.

"Brought you a big fish," he boomed in his deep voice.

Louie waved at Charlie, who had hooked the cable. He certainly had grown since he and Louie had parted. Now he was as tall as his father.

Charlie leapt over the gunwales.

"What'cha do'n, Louie?"

Louie remembered this favorite way of greeting but the voice saying it sounded more like Charlie's father's voice, deep throated and kind of raspy.

The two boys slapped each other on the back and gave each other their favorite crossed hand greeting. Sammy nudged his way in between them and pecked Charlie on the leg.

"Hey! Watch it, gull!" snapped Charlie. "What's with him?"

"Had a broken wing. Now he's my pet."

"Can't he fly now?"

"Think so. But he won't try."

"Hey, Charlie, how about getting your stuff?" Charlie's mother called from the dory's stern seat.

"We got to get going back." She threw a duffel to Charlie.

"Won't you stay and eat with us first and have a tour of the island?" asked Ma who by this time had come down from the house to greet their new arrivals.

"We'd like to but we left the other kids at home, so we need to be getting back 'afore the wind dies."

Charlie caught his duffel, as the dory slid down the tramway into the sea.

"See ye in a month," called Charlie's mother. "Don't go getting into no trouble now, ye hear!"

Louie helped Charlie take his duffel up to the house and to his loft bed room.

"We can see the whole island and reefs from here," Louie said, "also, from the lighthouse tower. Come on, I'll show you."

Charlie followed Louie through the shed up the lighthouse tower steps. Sammy followed both of them, causing the usual racket in the shed and the hens and rooster to scatter. The boys were too busy talking to take Sammy with them up the steps.

"Kuk! Kuk! Kuk!" Sammy flapped his good wing at the bottom of the steps.

After dinner Louie took Charlie around the island, showing him the ramp he was building for their double-ender and where the beach would be at low tide. They sat together under one of the evergreen trees and talked.

Sammy sat on a rock near them. His head hanging low.

Charlie pulled a package out of his pocket with cigarettes in it.

"Here, have one. All the kids are smoking 'em. I got this pack from off my pa's dresser when he was last out fishing."

Louie's pa had a pipe, but Louie didn't remember ever seeing him light it. It just hung from his mouth—sort of like a licorice stick.

"No, thanks," said Louie. "I don't like the smell."

"Ah, come on. All the kids are smoking 'em at school. Just try one. Won't hurt you."

Louie remembered that his pa had said that even if all the other kids were doing something he didn't have to do it too.

Louie watched as Charlie lit the cigarette and drew a long puff. "Ah . . . mellow." Charlie leaned back against the tree.

"Just try a drag," he handed the cigarette to Louie.

"Kuk! Kuk! Kuk!" Sammy screeched.

"I guess it won't hurt to take one drag," said Louie.

"Kuk! Kuk! Kuk!" Sammy flapped both his wings. Louie didn't notice. He coughed and gagged.

"Here," he gasped. He threw the cigarette back to Charlie as he stumbled to the nearest seaweed covered rock and vomited. He felt lightheaded.

Charlie put out the cigarette and followed him. "Hey, you'll get over that after smoking a few."

He slapped Louie on the back.

Pa was right, Louie thought. Even though Charlie was his best friend, he would not smoke another one of those and he hoped Charlie wouldn't either.

CHAPTER 19

Heavenly Host

That evening Louie wrote in the lighthouse log book:

August 1, 1903: *Wind SW, 5–10. Clear. Tipsy arrives bringing Charlie.*

Louie Hollander

After a supper of fish cakes, canned peas, and biscuits, Louie and Charlie arm wrestled and examined the new Boston Pilgrim baseball cards Charlie had brought with him.

"Wow! You have Bill Dineen and Cy Young!"

"Saw Cy Jones pitch once. Want one?"

"Gosh. Sure you want to part with it?"

"Sure. I know how to get others." Charlie winked and padded his pocket.

Louie picked the card of Bill Dineen.

"I'll read the Bible story tonight," said Louie's mother. She opened the Bible and read from Psalm 33:6.

"By the word of the Lord were the Heavens made.."

"Speaking of Heaven . . ." she looked out the window. "Just look at all those stars out tonight." She opened the door so that

Louie and Charlie could view the millions of twinkling lights dotting the darkened sky.

Louie and Charlie grabbed their bed quilts and went outside to find a comfortable spot among the bushes to lie on their backs and look up at the sky. They named the constellations they could see in the summer sky: The Big Dipper, Cassiopeia, and Scorpius. Sammy kept a safe distance and went to sleep with his beak under his mending wing.

When the lamps needed trimming in the tower, Louie's mother shooed them both upstairs to the loft.

"We're not tired," complained Charlie.

"You will be when the cock crows in the morning," she responded.

When she left to go to the tower, Louie and Charlie talked until the light from the beacon dancing off the walls and the waves dashing against the rocks lulled them both to sleep.

CHAPTER 20

Ready to Launch

Morning arrived too early.

Louie roused himself reluctantly when his mother called.

He poked Charlie who hid his head under the quilt.

"Coming? It's milking and egg collecting time."

Charlie had never milked a cow before and Betsy knew it.

More milk went on him than in the bucket! They both wolfed down scrambled eggs and corn bread before grabbing their fishing poles.

Fishing from a pier for little fish didn't appeal to Charlie. He had spent too many days on the *Tipsy* with her dories setting trawl lines and hauling in the big ones.

Bored, he put down his fishing pole and looked around for something else to do. He spied Sammy sitting on the piling nearby. He picked up a stone and threw it.

"Kuk! Kuk! Kuk!" Sammy flapped both wings and lifted himself off the piling just in time for the missile to whiz under him.

"I'll teach this bird to fly," he said and picked up another stone.

"Hey. Don't do that!" Louie said turning around.

"You'll hurt him."

"So what?"

Louie didn't like Charlie's tone. A chill went up his spine.

"Let's go back to the house. I think I heard Ma calling." Louie picked up Sammy who was shaking all over. He stroked his feathers until he calmed down and, still carrying Sammy, he went back to the house with his old friend.

Ma put them both to work painting the shutters on the windows. Around dinner time, they heard the familiar toot of the *Rainbow*.

"Ahoy, mates!" Captain Bowline shouted. "Found some more wood planks for your boat ramp."

Sure enough, two planks stuck out from the *Rainbow* launch's stern. Louie and Charlie helped Captain Bowline lift them up over the gunwales and then carried them up over the hill. They were just the right size to finish the ramp. After dinner the three of them worked to cement the planks in place along with an iron post placed just above the high tide mark. They placed the double-ender on the planks so that it rested in ready position at the top of the ramp and tied her to the post.

"Now ye're ready to take her out by yerselves for rowing and fishing," Captain Bowline said proudly.

But launching the double-ender had to wait. After morning chores, Ma wanted Louie and Charlie to collect driftwood and dried seaweed.

"Why can't we launch her to go rowing just for a short spell?" Louie pleaded.

"Because we need some kindling around here for starting the stove every day for cooking and to keep the house warm on foggy and damp days." Louie and Charlie obediently collected and piled the driftwood and seaweed near Betsy's shed.

After dinner Louie pleaded again.

"Can't we take her out now? I calculate there's little wind and no fog in sight."

"All right," said Ma, "but take this fog horn in case you need it."

Louie filled the jug, put his fishing pole and bucket of bait in the boat along with their cork life jackets and the small fog horn. Then the two boys slid her along the new ramp into the sea and climbed in, ready for their new adventure.

CHAPTER 21

Lost and Found

Keep in sight of the island. Expect you back by supper."
Ma waved good-bye to the two boys.

Louie stood to row the boat away from the beach and rock reefs rearing their ugly heads near the island. Charlie sat in the stern with his arms crossed—his legs stretching out to Louie's feet.

Sammy watched them go from a nearby rock and flapped his wings.

"Kuk! Kuk!"

"Bye, Sammy," called back Louie. "Take care of Ma."

As soon as the boat was clear of the treacherous rocks and out into the bay, Louie sat to row. He sang:

"Row, row, row your boat Gently down the stream.

Merrily, merrily, merrily, merrily Life is but a dream."

Charlie joined in to make it a round.

They passed a lobster man hauling in traps in a sloop. The sloop *Islanda* had an oblong shape, three sails, and a long bow sprit.

"Ahoy mates!" the man called, "nice day for row'n and fish'n."

"Name's Tom Shiver. What's yours?"

"Louie Hollander and Charlie Missen," Louie called back. "My ma and I are manning the light on Two Tree Island."

"A good thing there's a new keeper on that island. Been many wrecks on those rock ledges surrounding her."

"We'll keep her beacon burning," Louie assured him.

The *Islanda* sailed off to the next batch of lobster traps.

"Want to row for a while, Charlie, while I trawl for fish?"

"Okay."

Louie and Charlie carefully switched seats. Charlie dipped the oars deep into the water.

"Splash!"

He had forgotten to feather his wrists.

"Hey, leave the ocean out there," laughed Louie as he wiped the salt water from his face.

"Michael, row your boat ashore. Alleluia!" sang Louie.

"Louie, catch us a great big fish. Alleluia!"

"Charlie, row us out to sea. Alleluia!"

"Louie, . . . and they each tried to outdo the other with a new line.

They were so busy singing that Louie's fishing pole began to slip through his hands as the line tightened.

Louie grabbed the pole and brought the fish into the boat. "A mackerel!" he shouted.

"Charlie, row this boat ashore. Alleluia!"

"Look!" Charlie pointed over Louie's head. Like a cloud suddenly dropped from the sky, a white blanket of mist covered everything in its path.

"Man the oars. Head for shore!" Louie commanded.

"See if we can beat it. Here I'll take a turn."

He exchanged places with Charlie and rowed as hard as he could. He hoped Ma could tend the light and that the fog horn would work. He felt guilty being out here and not there to help.

They were still far from the island when the dense, dank fog covered them. They could see nothing but grey mist.

"What do we do now?" Charlie whined.

"Listen. That's our fog horn blowing. We need to toot our horn, too."

They took turns rowing and blowing through the long metal horn, whose high wailing sound carried on the wisps of the mist surrounding them.

Louie felt a growing ball of fear in his stomach.

He imagined them crashing onto a rock ledge. He wished his pa were here. But he had to be brave—for Charlie.

"Kuk! Kuk! Ha! Ha!"

Louie heard the sound before he saw him. At first he looked just like any other sea gull coming out of the grey mist. But instead of flying around their boat, the gull landed on the bow of the boat and flapped his wings.

"Sammy? Is that you?" Charlie stopped rowing and reached out to stroke the gull's feathers.

"You can fly!" Louie nearly capsized the boat he was so excited.

Sammy rose in the air and flew off in one direction into the mist and then returned.

"Kuk! Kuk! Ha! Ha!"

"I think he wants us to follow him," Charlie said.

Sammy's pattern continued. He flew ahead of them in a direction and came back to see if they were following.

When their boat rounded the spindle bell, the light beam became stronger. Louie stopped rowing and put his head on his hands.

"What's wrong?" asked Charlie. "You all right?"

"Just trying to focus my brain on recalling every detail of the chart in the lighthouse tower. I can just about estimate where the rock ledges are."

Louie turned to face the bow and row.

Sammy returned and stood on the bow and called, "Kuk! Kuk! Kuk!"

Sammy's beak pierced through the fog and he lifted one wing. Louie spotted the familiar rock ledge and steered in the direction away from Sammy's pointed wing. The fog horn from the island sounded close.

With Sammy's high-pitched calling and pointing his wing in the direction of each rock ledge and with Louie's expert rowing they rounded the head of the island.

"There's the ramp!" yelled Charlie, "and your Ma." Louie threw his mother the painter and she guided the boat onto the ramp.

"Sammy brought us home safely," Louie told her.

Both boys let her hug them. Meanwhile, Sammy had spied the fish in the bottom of the boat. He would have eaten it all, but Charlie grabbed it and took it into the house.

Feathering: means turning your wrists so that the oar blades lie parallel to the surface of the water when bringing them back after pulling them through the water.

CHAPTER 22

Fogbound

This supper sure tastes good." Charlie told Louie's mother. She had made mashed potatoes to go with the fish.

"Ma, were you worried about us?"

"Sometimes. That fog came on so suddenly. Then I prayed that God would bring you home safely. Sammy must have gotten the message."

The three turned to look at Sammy who was picking happily at the cooked mackerel on Louie's plate.

"Hey, save some for me," Louie pushed Sammy gently away, "that dark part's my favorite."

"Here, have some mashed potatoes." Charlie shoved his plate toward Sammy.

By the end of the meal, mashed potatoes almost covered Sammy's face.

"Hi, Santa Claus Sammy."

"Ha! Ha! Ha!" the gull replied.

For the remainder of the night, Louie and Charlie tended the beacon while Louie's mother slept. Sammy flapped his wings and flew out into the grey mist.

The fog horn's mournful sound hounded them day in and day out. Louie wrote in the lighthouse log each day either "fog in" or "fog hovering."

All three of them were on ready alert. Usually around late morning sun broke through and pushed the fog bank out to sea but every evening it returned.

Louie and Charlie worked up an appetite going up and down the lighthouse tower steps to refuel the lamp reservoir, turn the lamp, clean the lens and windows, or wind the winch for the fog horn and stoke the fog horn engine.

Sammy came to sit on the lighthouse catwalk railing to look out into the fog and then back at the boys. Sometimes he flew away then he flew back. When he returned, he "kukked" loudly or pecked on a window. Louie never knew when to expect his reappearance.

"I guess he's like you when you first left for school," Ma said, "You wanted to go, but you cried when you left and hugged me when you got home."

Hug, ugh, thought Louie. But he understand what Ma meant.

When they weren't tending the light or horn or doing daily chores, Louie and Charlie invented games. For one game, they threw an old can offshore and hit it with pebbles until it sank. They built a stone launcher out of driftwood. Charlie had by now given up throwing pebbles and stones at birds. He had a greater respect for birds since Sammy had rescued them in the fog.

Fog kept them damp but did not refill the cisterns. They had to use some of the water in the jugs that Captain Bowline had brought them.

"Better to conserve again," Louie's mother cautioned.

Water, water all around us but not a drop to drink, thought Louie. How would they survive if the drought continued?

CHAPTER 23

Anticipation

Each new tide carried surprises.

Louie and Charlie explored the island at low tides. They found a few star fish but mostly periwinkle snails, limpets, hermit crabs, mussels, and broken shells. The sea yielded its share of bottles and cans as well as buoys.

"Buoys remind me of the *Islanda* we saw while we were out rowing and fishing the other day," Charlie commented.

"Wonder whether he made it in before the fog hit?"

"Ever been sailing?" Charlie asked. "No, ain't." Louie replied.

"Sure would like to ride on that bow sprit, though."

By the end of the week, a weather pattern from the west had brought in a 10–15 knot westerly wind that carried the hovering fog bank clear out to sea.

The *Rainbow* arrived with a load of hay, some fresh water, and cans of food. Louie, Charlie, and Ma helped empty each launch load Captain Bowline brought up the ramp.

"Missus thought ye'd like some more fresh veg'tables and fruit so she gave me these to give ye."

"Great. Thanks." Louie said, "Better than eating out of cans And our garden hadn't produced any vegetables—just a few blueberries from the bushes."

"Did you ever meet Captain Shiver?" Louie asked him.

"Yep. Know him well. Buys me lobsters from him."

"If you see his boat *Islanda*, tell him Louie and Charlie said hi. Maybe he'd like us to show him around the lighthouse tower when he's passing by."

"Sure thing. Now got to get going. Fog's kept me from checking on the buoys, bells, and spars."

Louie and Charlie went up to the lighthouse tower catwalk to wave goodbye to the *Rainbow* as it pulled away. As far as the eye could see, sailboats dotted the horizon.

"Some big yachts," commented Charlie, "must be summer folk."

"Wish I'd had Pa's spy glass so I could see them better."

"I wonder if one of them is *Islanda*," Charlie added.

Bow Sprit: Wooden spar that sticks out from the bow of some sloops, sometimes carrying two sails.

CHAPTER 24

Sail Ho

They didn't have to wonder long.

After dinner, as Charlie and Louie were roaming the island for fresh treasures, they noticed a gaff-rigged sloop coming toward them.

"Ahoy, mates!" called a voice from *Islanda* as she drew close to the pier. There were two persons in the sloop—Captain Shiver and a boy about Charlie's height.

"Hear yer offering a tour of the lighthouse."

"How about a tour in exchange for a sail?"

Captain Shiver and the boy tied up the *Islanda* on the mooring and dropped her sails. Louie and Charlie winched her double-ender up onto the tramway so the two could disembark.

"This here's my son, Will. He minds the sails when I'm lobster'n."

"Will, this here's Louie and Charlie. They was out a fur piece when that fog hit." He turned to Louie.

"Glad your light and fog horn was working or wouldn't have made it back meself."

Louie and Charlie took Captain Shiver and Will to the house and introduced them to his mother.

"They invited us to go sailing with them, after we show them the lighthouse tower. Can we?"

"I guess I can spare you for a few hours." Louie's mother winked at Captain Shiver.

Louie led Will and Captain Shiver up the lighthouse steps and gave them a complete tour of the tower. He also showed them how the beacon worked.

"It's my job to clean the lens and lamp jet, wind the clockwork mechanism, and polish the brass," Louie said proudly.

"Charlie's here visiting and helping for the rest of the summer."

"Quite a job," said Captain Shiver. "Yer ma must be right proud of ye." Louie blushed.

"And he even has a pet sea gull, Sammy, who brought us safely back to this island during that fog," added Charlie.

"Gulls are right smart. But they ain't learned not to mess on me deck." They all laughed.

After the tour, Louie's mother gave them some cookies she had made. Then she lowered the cable for the double-ender to make its way back to the sloop. Will took Captain Shiver out first and then returned for Charlie and Louie.

"Be ready to set sail soon's I cast her off," Captain Shiver commanded. He gave Louie and Charlie each a halyard for the staysail and jib and told them when to pull on them. He told Will to pay out the main so as to catch the wind and take the sloop away from the mooring.

Soon *Islanda* was sailing away in the breeze, heeling just the right amount.

"Who'd like to get wet first?" asked Captain Shiver. Louie thought he meant go overboard when the wind heeled the boat over so he climbed to the high side.

Will clarified, "he means ride the bowsprit."

Louie looked at the white foam passing by him. He really didn't want to go swimming.

"Not much to it," Will said, "Just have to hold on to the spar and put your feet on the stay—like a broom stick."

"Here. I'll go first. You watch."

"Wow," said Louie when it came to his turn. The bowsprit dipped then rose above the waves.

More like riding a bucking broncho, he thought. The wind whipped past the back of the filled sails, the lines taunt.

"Ride 'em cowboy," he said to nobody.

Charlie tried to hold onto the bowsprit from underneath and they almost lost him overboard.

Louie liked sitting by the tiller and steering the sloop with Captain Shiver's help.

Will and Charlie trimmed the sails and they all joined in singing Sea Shanties:

"Come all ye young fellows that follows the sea
To me, way hey, blow the man down
Now please pay attention and listen to me
Give me some time to blow the man down."

and

"Away, haul away, Oh, haul and sing together,
Away haul away, Haul away, Joe!
Oh, once I had an Irish girl, but she was fat and lazy,
Away haul away, Haul away, Charlie!
And then I had yeller girl, she nigh druv me crazy,
Away haul away, Haul away, Louie!
But now I've got a Yankee girl, and she is just a daisy.
Away haul away, Haul away, Will!"

All too soon it was time to head back to Two Tree Island. Since the tide had ebbed Louie suggested that Captain Shiver head for the lee-low side of the island. When Islanda rounded the point, they saw Ma rowing out to meet them in their double-ender.

"I was afraid you'd make sailors of them before they'd mastered lighthouse tending," she joked as the Louie and Charlie transferred into their rowboat.

"Come back soon!" the two boys called in unison as *Islanda* sailed on her way.

Someday, thought Louie, I'd like to own one of those sloops.

Lines: Ropes on a sailboat. Each line has a purpose. Halyards pull up sails. Sheets let them in and out.

Sails: Main sail is the biggest. Stay sail is next. Jib is the smallest.

Bow: Front of boat.

Stern: Rear of boat.

Starboard: Right side of boat facing bow.

Port: Left side of boat facing bow.

Heeling: Wind pushes boat over to one side.

Trim the Sails: Pull them in.

Pay out the sails: Let them out.

Cast off: Go away from a wharf or dock by releasing painter.

Stay: Metal strip that bolts the mast and spars to the boat's deck.

Spar: wooden support like a mast or a gaff.

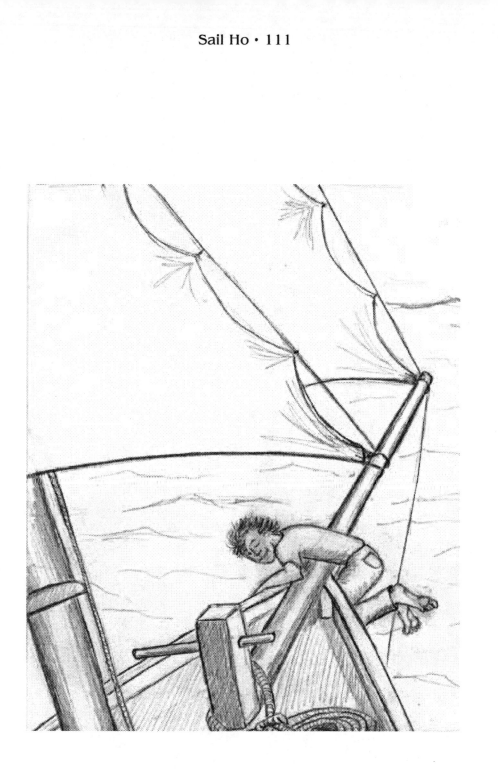

CHAPTER 25

More Temptation

Charlie still smoked. Louie could tell.

Instead of fishing from the wharf in the morning, Charlie disappeared. Louie hated how he smelled when he returned.

"I'll show you something special if you don't tell anyone," Charlie teased Louie one night as they were getting ready for bed. "Promise?"

Charlie pulled out another pack of cigarettes from his duffel bag.

"Promise." agreed Louie.

Charlie took out a card from the pack and showed it to Louie.

"This brand has these special cards." He put one under Louie's nose.

On the card was a picture of a scantily clad woman. Charlie tried to turn his head away. He'd never seen so much of a woman's body before. Louie wondered what kind of a woman would allow her picture to be taken with so few clothes on and allow her photo to be put in a pack of cigarettes.

Louie knew he shouldn't look, but it was hard not to with Charlie sticking the card in his face. He cleared his throat, tightened his muscles, and changed the subject.

"Wish you wouldn't smoke those things. Ma might find out and send you home."

"If you must smoke them," Louie sighed, "smoke away from the house and throw your matches and burnt cigarettes into the ocean. Lighting anything on this island where there is kerosene stored is dangerous."

His mother had told him never to light a match except in the house to light the stove or in the tower to light the lamp. Louie knew she would be furious if she found out about Charlie's smoking.

"Night, Charlie."

Louie turned over on his side away from the flickering light and slept. A breeze that billowed the curtains in the dormer window lifted his worries and carried them away. Yet, he had another one of those dreams where he thought he heard his pa calling.

CHAPTER 26

Brothers

August 8, 1903: *Mackerel sky two days dry. Wind shift to west. Barometer reads VERY DRY. Islanda visited yesterday.*

Molly Hollander

Must be hot inland." Louie's mother commented at break-fast the next day.

"They probably need rain, too. She had put on her best skirt and blouse.

"Missed Reverend Hornblower last week, because of the fog. Hope he'll come today," she sighed.

Louie took his fishing pole and went down to the pier to wait for the fish to bite. He called for Sammy but Sammy had not returned from his latest flight. Louie missed him.

"Whatcha' do'n?" Charlie appeared at his side smelling of smoke again.

"What were you doing?" Charlie turned back to his fishing feeling angry.

Just then they heard the familiar, "Ahoy, mates!"

The *Rainbow* launch chugged up to the pier. Louie's mood lightened when he spied Uncle Sam.

"Missus couldn't come 'cause Harry's got the fever."

"Reckon it'll just be the five of us worshiping.

We'll sing real loud!" said Captain Bowline.

"I brought you both harmonicas," said Uncle Sam.

He gave one each to Louie and Charlie as the four of them climbed up the steep steps to the house.

"Where's Sammy?"

"Flew away." Louie pointed out to sea to the gulls in the distance.

"Guess you must have loved him so much he felt free to leave."

Uncle Sam put his arm around Louie.

"What have you two been up to?"

Louie told him all about being lost in the fog and Sammy guiding them back to the island and their sail on *Islanda* with Captain Shiver. Charlie scowled as he walked up the steps far behind them.

"And this is the famous Charlie, I've been hearing so much about." Uncle Sam stopped, turned to Charlie, and waited for him to come alongside.

Ma settled them in the parlor. Then they sang hymns. Uncle Sam asked Louie to read the Bible lesson. Afterwards Uncle Sam retold the story.

"Two brothers lived with their father on a big estate. The younger brother asked his father for his inheritance. His father gave him the money. He went away and spent it all on smoking, drinking, and prostitutes. When he was sick and tired of living like a pig, he decided to go back home and tell his pa how sorry he was. His pa saw him coming back away far off so he ran to meet him, gave him a hug, and welcomed him home with a feast. Now the older brother got really angry. He had stayed at home all that time and had lived just the way his father and mother had wanted him to. Yet no feast had been given in his honor!"

"Which brother do you think the father loved best?"

Louie felt like Charlie's old brother sometimes, even though Charlie was older than Louie. He wondered though if Charlie got the story.

"I think the younger brother," said Charlie.

"He loved both of them," said Uncle Sam, "but his love was so great that he forgave all the bad things the younger brother had done when he said he was sorry."

Ma had cooked a ham hock. She had made mashed potatoes and cooked some green beans. She had even made a deep dish blueberry pie for desert.

"Want to hear some exciting news?"

Four heads turned to Uncle Sam, and eight ears tuned in.

"Last week I took the steamer to Bath and then the Central, the train to Boston, to watch the Boston Pilgrims play baseball against the Philadelphia Phillies. The Pilgrims are now in the lead for the American League pennant."

"Wow!" Louie said. "What was it like?"

"The steamer, train ride, or the game?"

"All."

"Well, it took us eighteen hours by steamer and train. Weather was rough and I thought the steamer would capsize any moment. Lots of folks were seasick. Had to wait in Bath for the Central and then, when we got to the station outside of Boston, it was another half day by buggy to the Huntington Avenue Grounds. It was a long, hot trip but worth it."

"Who pitched?" Charlie sat on the edge of his seat.

"Did you catch any balls?"

"Deenan pitched and only gave up four hits and one run. Buck Freeman led off with a triple and Freddy Parent reached base on an error, with Freeman holding third. Candy LaChance then sacrificed Parent to second. Hobe Ferris followed with a double. The score was 11–6."

Uncle Sam reached in his pocket and brought out a baseball. "Got some autographs on this one."

He passed the ball around. Louie and Charlie examined it carefully.

"You can keep it."

"Thank you!" Louie leapt out of his chair and gave Uncle Sam a hug. Charlie stood and fingered the ball.

After dinner Louie and Charlie walked around the island with Uncle Sam and Captain Bowline. Louie sat down on a rock to talk to Uncle Sam while Charlie and Captain Bowline examined the tide pools and rock crevices for sea life.

"About that Bible story you read . . ." Louie began.

"Yes?" Uncle Sam listened.

"Well, I sometimes feel like Charlie's older brother, especially when he smokes and shows me pictures of near naked women."

"Go on."

"We used to have fun together—like brothers. But now he's trying to get me to do things that don't seem like fun. Some of them seem—well–bad."

"Is he pressuring you?"

"Sometimes."

"You're trying not to but you want him to like you and you want to still like him."

"Yeah."

"In the Bible story the Father loved both his sons, even though one did bad things. But he couldn't help the son who did bad things until he repented and returned home to ask for his father's forgiveness. Doesn't sound like Charlie is ready to do that, yet. It's okay to feel angry like the older brother."

Some of the anger and frustration with Charlie left Louie after he talked to Uncle Sam. Charlie returned with Captain Bowline.

"We found an osprey nest!"

"Board'n time," Captain Bowline announced.

That night Louie dreamt he hit a home run.

CHAPTER 27

Painting and Swimming

G ood day for whitewashing the tower." Louie's mother announced at breakfast.

"With two of you, shouldn't take you long."

"Just like Tom Sawyer and Huck Finn," Louie responded.

After chores, Louie and Charlie put on old torn shirts that reached
down and covered most of their pants. With a bucket of whitewash
in one hand and brush in the other, they set to work on the tower.

"Which book was your favorite?" Louie asked Charlie, "Tom
Sawyer or Huckleberry Finn?"

"I liked the one about Huck Finn the best. His pa was just like
my pa."

"What do you mean?"

"His pa was always getting drunk and beating him up. My pa
goes to the bar when he gets home from a long fishing spell. Then
he gets mean and hits Ma, me, and my sister. He used to go after my
older brother, but he's bigger then him now. We all just wished he
stay away in his fishing boat."

"Must be awful." Louie took a long stroke of his paint brush.

"Yeah. Glad Ma let me come here. It keeps getting worse at
home."

The two boys painted in silence. Louie thought he understood Charlie better now. His pa hadn't been mean like that.

Louie's mother came out to inspect their work.

"Looks good. Want to take a break for some food."

"I'm starving, Mrs. Hollander," Charlie said. "Thought ye'd never ask."

"How does clam chowder, fish cakes, and fresh biscuits sound?"

"I could eat a horse," Charlie said.

"No horse on the island—just hens and a cow."

"Can we let some of the eggs hatch so we could have chicken to eat once in a while, Ma?" Louie asked.

"Not a bad idea. Just leave a few eggs under each hen next time you collect them. Eating just fish and meat from cans does get boring."

Louie and Charlie nodded in agreement.

"Can we try swimming off the beach?" Louie asked. "The tide's out and with as hot as it's been I bet the water is warmer."

Louie's mother agreed and came down to the shore to sit on a rock and sew while Louie and Charlie swam. They ran in, took a few strokes, and ran back out.

"Ha! Ha! Ha!" Sammy flew in over their heads and swooped down into the water to nip their toes. Each time one of them would try to catch him, Sammy just slipped through their fingers and flew up. They grabbed and splashed. Sammy eluded them each time.

Turning blue, teeth chattering, Louie and Charlie finally gave up and lay down on a hot rock to dry.

When they went back in the house to dress, Charlie took a cigarette and matches out of the pack in his duffel.

"I'm going back to painting. See you later." Louie said as Charlie disappeared.

CHAPTER 28

Fire

M oo! Moo!"

Wonder what Betsy's fussing about?

Louie turned his head away from the tower and caught a glimpse of Charlie running around the side of the house calling, "Fire! Come quick!"

Louie grabbed his paint bucket. "Where?"

Charlie pointed and Louie followed.

"Ma!" he called as he ran by. Ma came out of the front door wiping her hands on her apron.

"What's wrong?" She followed the two boys around the side of the house.

She gasped when she saw it. Smoke billowed from the rear of the cow shed.

"Get Betsy out of there!" She yelled.

Charlie reached the shed first. He grabbed Betsy by her bridle. He tried to yank her out, but she wouldn't budge.

"Moo! Moo! Moo!" She bellowed.

Louie ran up beside Charlie.

"Come on, Betsy," he coaxed.

He, too, grabbed Betsy's bridle.

"It's ok," he said in a calm voice to Betsy.

Flames flickered from the back of the shed.

Smoke came from Betsy's tail. She tossed her rear hooves.

Using their combined strength, Louie and Charlie pulled Betsy from the flaming shed.

Louie took off his shirt.

"Hold her still!" He said to Charlie.

Louie wrapped his shirt around Betsy's tail while Charlie held her bridle with one hand and stroked her back with the other. Betsy kicked Louie.

"Ouch!" Louie cried, jumping back just as one wild hoof grazed his leg. Blood gushed out.

"Take Betsy over there!" Ma yelled at Charlie, pointing to the two trees.

She pulled off her apron and tied it around the bleeding gash in Louie's leg. She picked up Louie's bucket and dumped the paint out onto the ground.

"Can you make it up to the house to get another bucket?" She asked him. "I'll fill this one with sea water."

"Sure, Ma," Louie replied. He hopped and limped back to the house.

"Don't just stand there, Charlie," Ma shouted at Charlie, "go help."

"And bring some rope to tie Betsy," she added as she ran to the burning shed and doused it with water.

Charlie ran back with another bucket. Louie half ran, half hopped behind him with a rope.

Charlie joined Ma at the sea's edge.

Louie found Betsy running in circles and pawing the ground near the two trees. He caught her bridle and tied her with the rope to one of the trees.

Then he stood by the shed while Ma filled the buckets. She handed them to Charlie who ran with them to Louie. Louie tossed them on the now blazing shed.

"Move back, Louie!" shouted Ma over the noise of the roaring flames.

Louie jumped back as one side of the shed collapsed just inches from his feet.

"Need to keep it from spreading!" Ma called again.

"Douse the area around the shed with water! Move that driftwood."

Louie threw each bucket of sea water Charlie brought to him on the grass around the shed. He pulled the driftwood away from the shed.

They were so busy they barely noticed the few drops of water that were beginning to fall from the heavens. As the rain picked up it finally doused the fire. The remains of the shed sizzled and then lay charred and ruined.

Louie, Charlie, and Ma put down their buckets and surveyed the damage.

"Moo. Moo." Betsy reminded them she was still alive.

"Move her over to the boathouse shed," Ma said, "Then come back up to the house and get dried off."

"I'll tend that gash," she nodded to Louie.

Back inside Ma gathered some rags and collected the iodine from the medicine chest.

After moving Betsy and getting her settled in her new shed, Louie and Charlie returned to the house. They were drenched and covered with soot.

"Go up, wash, and change," she ordered Charlie, "and bring down some dry clothes for Louie." She carefully untied her blood soiled apron from Louie's leg and looked at the gash in his leg.

"Does it hurt to lift your leg and move your foot?" she asked Louie.

Louie winced as he raised his damaged leg and bent his ankles.

"Ouch!" he said as Ma washed his wound and put iodine on it. "That hurts more than moving my leg."

"Well you better keep it elevated and rest it for awhile," she told him. She felt the bone. "No breaks. Just bruised, I think."

As soon as both Louie and Charlie had put on dry clothes Ma brought them both some hot cocoa.

"How did the fire start?" She looked right at Charlie.

Charlie shuffled his feet, clenched and unclenched his hands, and lowered his head. He moved the hot cocoa from one hand to another.

"I . . . I . . . think I started it Ma'am. But please don't send me home. My pa will kill me."

"Okay, Charlie, calm down. No one's talking about sending you home. Sit down and tell me how it happened."

"I was having a smoke," Charlie's voice was barely audible. "Louie told me to throw the match and cigarette into the sea after I put them out. Well I think one of them landed in the pile of dried seaweed by the shed instead. Guess, I didn't put it all the way out. I'm sorry."

Louie's mother furrowed her brow. She took a deep breath and let it out slowly. Then she said, "You won't smoke any more cigarettes while you're here with us, will you?"

"No, Ma'am."

"You'll help rebuild the shed, won't you?"

"Yes, Ma'am."

"Guess we don't have to tell your parents, then."

"Thank you, Ma'am!" This time it was Charlie who gave Ma a hug.

CHAPTER 29

Resentment

Ma hoisted the SOS flag.

"Don't know if anyone will come until this storm lets up but if a ship goes by the lighthouse and sees the flag they'll pass the distress signal along to the Lighthouse Service Board," she told Louie.

"The nurse should come and look at your leg," she continued. "We also need the Lighthouse Service's help in rebuilding the shed, more straw for Betsy, feed for the hens, food supplies, and more whitewash."

Because the storm had picked up intensity and the visibility was poor, the light beacon needed constant tending so that it stayed on day and night.

After a day of rest, Louie managed to hobble around enough to help Ma with the light beacon as well as winch and stock the fog horn engine with coal.

Ma asked Charlie to help, but he complained of a headache and nausea. Most of the time he lay on his bed and read the *Adventures of Huckleberry Finn*. Ma gave him some castor oil.

Some feast, thought Louie.

Betsy didn't like her new quarters so her mooing added to the moaning of the fog horn.

"A chorus," said Louie as he picked up his new harmonica and added its sounds as the accompanying orchestra.

Louie didn't have the time or the inclination to feel sorry for Charlie. Even though his leg still hurt, he couldn't lie around like Charlie. He knew he had to be strong and alert to help man the lighthouse. He still resented Charlie for starting the fire and burning up the shed.

"Smoke-up!" yelled Ma. She ran through the shed to the tower. Louie limped behind her. They could both see the flame at the top of the tower. When they reached the lamp, smoke and soot were all over the place.

Ma turned off the kerosene so the flame went out.

"Quick, Louie, hand me that other lamp. It won't shine for twelve miles like the other lamp but it'll have to do until we can clean up this place."

"Must have been some dirt in the lamp jet." She removed the jet after it had cooled down enough to handle.

Ma went down the stairs to fill a bucket with water from a cistern. The cisterns had filled enough to spare a bucket of fresh water. When Ma returned, Louie took a rag and cleaned the inside of the tower windows while Ma cleaned the prisms on the Fresnel lens. Louie polished the brass. It took them over an hour.

"At least the fog horn still works," Ma said.

When they had cleaned up all the soot, Ma relit the jet and Louie wound the clockwork for the beacon. By then it was time to stoke the coals that made the steam for the fog horn.

Louie and Ma tended the lamp and fog horn through the night, four hours on and four hours off. Charlie lay on his bed and moaned.

Join the chorus, Louie thought as he dosed off to Charlie's moaning and the mournful sound of the fog horn, the wind whistling in the two trees, and the waves dashing their fury against the rocks.

Smoke-up: When kerosene in a lamp jet burns like liquid giving off large amounts of smoke and flame; caused by small pieces of dirt clogging the jet.

CHAPTER 30

Redemption

W ake up!" Ma shook Louie. "Your shift."

Louie dragged himself out of bed, put on his oil-skin jacket over his pajamas and pulled on his boots. By now, he was so numb he didn't even feel the throbbing in his leg anymore. He rubbed the sleep from his eyes, doused some water on his face, and trudged his way through the shed up the lighthouse tower steps.

"Rotate the beacon clockwork—fill the reservoir—empty the dust pan—check the fog horn." He now knew the routine by heart.

"The wind seems to have let up," he said when he stuck his head outside.

He checked the log book. Ma had been making the entries since Charlie had arrived.

August 15, 1903 - *Wind NE. Stormy: wind and rain. Fire destroyed cow shed. Put up SOS flag. No ships in sight.*

Molly Hollander

Louie didn't think that any ships had seen the SOS flag because of the storm.

Now he felt the throbbing in his bad leg. All his bones ached. Even his back hurt. Is this what they mean by growing pains? He wondered. If so, he wished he could lie down, too—like Charlie—and have Ma fuss over him instead of growing up to be a man!

By morning the storm had diminished and some visibility had returned. Louie checked the level of the water in the cisterns and found that the rain had filled them again.

He added milking Betsy to his list of chores because Charlie still complained of his stomach hurting and his head aching. In between shifts at the lighthouse tower, Ma had managed to fix Charlie a cup of tea and give him some more castor oil. Louie's resentment grew.

Around noon, a steamer tooted her whistle and rang her bell as she passed. Within three hours Louie could see the *Rainbow* on the horizon heading for the island.

"Ahoy!" called out Captain Bowline. He made the tender fast at the mooring and let down the launch from its davit. Out from the coaming three slickered heads appeared.

"Heard ye was in trouble." Captain Bowline shouted through a megaphone.

"Brought the nurse. Her name's Fanny Figgins. Thought someone was sick."

"Someone is," Ma answered as she started the engine to winch the cable down into the angry sea.

It took the *Rainbow*'s launch two tries and some swift maneuvering to slide onto the tramway. By this time, Louie had joined Ma. They both worked on the winch to haul the launch up out of the churning sea. Louie was glad to see Uncle Sam, the first out of the boat to help. Captain Bowline returned to the *Rainbow* to pick up the other two passengers.

"Got here as fast as we could when we heard you were flying the SOS flag," Mr. McAllister said when he arrived on the next trip.

"What's the problem?" Nurse Figgins, who followed him out of the launch, asked Ma.

"Well, Louie hurt his leg rescuing Betsy from the burning cow shed and . . ." she began as they carefully climbed up the slippery rock steps. Ma had told them the whole story by the time they reached the pile of wet ashes that had been the shed.

"Lucky Charlie wasn't smoking near the kerosene tank," Mr. McAllister sighed.

"I'll send some lumber and a crew to rebuild it."

"Charlie agreed to help and not to smoke on this island again," Ma said.

"Think I know why he's feeling poorly, now," Uncle Sam said. He nodded to Nurse Figgins. "But first let's look at your leg, Louie."

Nurse Figgins examined Louie's leg. She noted the bruises around the cut that had begun to heal. "No break. Just a bad bone bruise." She changed the dressing.

"Now let's see to Charlie. He needs to help more around here so you can rest that leg." Nurse Figgins beckoned to Uncle Sam. The two of them climbed up to the loft to see Charlie, who had not come down to the pier when the *Rainbow* arrived.

Mr. McAllister sat with Louie and his ma in the parlor. Ma praised Louie's efforts to rescue Betsy from the fire and to help her man the lighthouse beacon and fog horn.

"Fine job." Mr. McAllister said to Louie. Then, he added, "I have some news for you both."

He continued, "I talked to the Lighthouse Service Board when we met last week . . ."

Louie wondered what was said at that meeting. Probably they didn't want a woman manning Two Tree Island lighthouse, even with his help.

Mr. McAllister continued, "I recommended that they make your job here as Two Tree Island lighthouse keepers permanent."

Ma's eyebrows went up and her mouth opened wide into a big grin. "Thank you, Mr. McAllister. We appreciate your confidence in us."

Louie was speechless.

Mr. McAllister turned to Louie. "Now about rebuilding that shed. How much lumber do you think we'll need?"

Louie felt a foot taller. Mr. McAllister had asked for his opinion—man to man! He took a deep breath, then asked, "Think you could build us a boat house, too, near the new ramp for the dory? We could use the other shed near the pier to store coal when it comes on the gundalow this fall."

"Good idea, Louie," Mr. McAllister replied.

"Don't know why the Board didn't build it over there in the first place. Better landing site. I'll check the government budget tomorrow. See if the Service can afford to build two sheds. Don't see why not long as the crew is working. Just a bit more lumber that's all. Now let's see if we can calculate the amount.."

Just then, Nurse Figgins came down the stairs from the loft without Uncle Sam.

"No fever," she announced, "hard to quit smoking cold turkey. Brain and body need to adjust."

She turned to Ma. "You've been right kind to him—lots of castor oil and sympathy. Now he needs to be up helping around here. Rev. Hornblower will be a little while yet. I'll just sit here by the stove and dry off. Got wet on the way out."

While Mr. McAllister and Ma figured on lumber quantity, Louie made his way through the shed and slowly up the lighthouse tower steps. "Might as well look to the lamp," he said to the hens as he passed.

He didn't call me son this time and Ma and I are a lighthouse manning team. Wow! He thought as he filled a can with kerosene and lugged it up the lighthouse tower steps. His wariness toward Mr. McAllister lessened with each step.

He spent the next hour tending the lamp and cleaning the brass. His ears were now attuned to all the sounds in the lighthouse tower.

"Something is missing," he said to nobody.

Somebody answered, "The rain has stopped."

Louie turned to find Uncle Sam standing behind him.

"Look. Barometer now points to *CHANGE*."

Charlie turned to look at Uncle Sam, then back to the barometer. They both walked out to the catwalk to look out to sea.

"Fair weather ahead," they said in unison.

Steamer: a coal fired boat emitting steam.

Coaming: A raised frame around a hatchway on the deck of a ship to keep out water.

CHAPTER 31

Restoration

The launch with her passengers chugged back to the *Rainbow* late that afternoon.

The sea had calmed down so the launch made a smoother exit than entrance. Mr. Mcallister called back that the lighthouse tender would return in a few days with a working crew, lumber, and supplies.

Louie stopped the fog horn as soon as the sky began to clear, but, with evening approaching, kept the beacon burning. He milked and unbridled Betsy so she could nibble on the sea grass.

Finally, he went up to the loft to rest his leg.

"Hi Louie, watch'a do'n?" Charlie asked.

"How you do'n?" responded Louie.

"Better. That preacher-man is okay."

"You sure had a long talk," Louie wanted to ask what they talked about, but couldn't get up nerve.

"Ayuh. We shared stories."

"What about?" There, he'd said it.

"Lots of stuff. Mostly about what it's like growing up, 'specially with a mean pa."

"You mean Uncle Sam's pa was mean, too?" Louie asked.

"Yep. Just like mine. When his pa drowned at sea, he had lots of mixed feelings. He was hurting so bad—angry at God, too—he started smoking and drinking. Got in real trouble."

"What kind of trouble?" Louie was all ears.

"Got in a fight. Hauled off to jail."

"Uncle Sam?"

"Yep. Some temperance folks came to the jail and converted him. He took an oath swearing never to drink or smoke again. Told me his head and stomach ached so bad he didn't know whether he'd make it. Said God helped him through the worst. He and I prayed then. I asked God to help me. Feel lots better, now."

The two boys gave each other the familiar crossed arm greeting and called down the stairs.

"What's for supper? We're starving!"

"Come down and see," Ma called back.

The three of them bowed their heads as Ma prayed, "Thank you, Lord, for this food, good health, and fair weather." Then Louie and Charlie devoured several helpings of her fish chowder and newly baked molasses cake.

Charlie went with Louie to the top of the tower to tend the light and write in the logbook.

Sunday, August 16,1903: *Stormy; rain; poor visibility. Kept beacon on and fog horn working. Lighthouse Board Officer, Mr. McAllister, comes on Rainbow with Nurse Figgins, and Reverend Hornblower in response to SOS. Molly Hollander becomes permanent lighthouse keeper. Barometer reads CHANGE.*

Louie Hollander

CHAPTER 32

Rebuilding

The next morning Louie felt as fresh as the breeze. He wanted to crow with the rooster. Even his bruised leg didn't ache anymore.

He had time to roam the island with Charlie while they waited for the lighthouse tender to return. They collected driftwood and whittled some birds with Louie's knife. One day at low tide, they discovered a rock crevice that led down through a narrow opening into a larger space with a sandy bottom. Some crabs, minnows, and a live lobster were caught in a salt water pool. Carefully grabbing the lobster behind his claws and putting the crabs in one of their shirts, they exited with their catch from their newly discovered rock cave just as the tide began to fill it up again.

On Wednesday the lighthouse tender arrived, bringing a crew of two workmen and some lumber as well as the supplies Ma had ordered. Charlie and Louie helped them unload.

Then Charlie, true to his word, joined the men in rebuilding the shed for Betsy. He even helped them construct the new boat shed. Louie fished and tended to lighthouse keeping chores for Ma.

The men stayed for a week and worked on building the sheds waiting for the Lighthouse tender to return. Ma kept busy during the day preparing meals for all of them. Louie helped her set up cots in the empty bedroom for the crew for sleeping.

Because Charlie worked every day helping with the building of the sheds, after chores Louie had time to explore for more sea life around the island. One day he found two seals sunning themselves on low lying rocks.

"Arf! Arf! the seals barked, lifting webbed fins as if waving at him.

One of the seals slid back into the ocean when Louie came closer. But the other seal didn't move.

I wonder if he's injured? Louie thought.

He cautiously made his way toward the seal. It lifted one webbed fin and then the other, but made no move back toward the sea.

"Here, feller. Won't hurt you," Louie beckoned the seal to come closer.

"Arf? Arf?" the seal cocked his head and twitched his whiskers.

Louie reached out to stroke his wet skin lightly. The seal turned and nudged Louie's arm, then slowly slid back into the sea.

"Bye feller. Come back and see me again," Louie waved as the seal swam away, his head barely skimming the surface of the water.

Charlie took breaks from working on building the sheds to join Louie in watching for the seals to return. The two boys explored all the island rocks where seals might sun themselves, looking seaward for their shiny heads to appear.

CHAPTER 33

Return

I nstead of seals, they spied the *Tipsy* returning.

"No, it can't be!" Charlie moaned when he saw the familiar fishing schooner. "It's not time for them to come."

"Yes. It is. It's the end of August and school starts soon," Ma said coming up behind him and putting her arm around his shoulders.

She continued, "and you've become a master builder."

"Gosh darn," Louie added, "we've hardly had any time to-gether."

"There'll be other times, Louie," Ma replied. She walked down the steep hill and waved to the figures on the schooner. They waved back.

"*Tipsy*, ahoy! Can you come around the other side of the island to anchor?" Ma called through a megaphone. "We've got a better landing site over there, now."

Four figures trimmed lines and turned the schooner so that she headed toward the lee side of the island. There she dropped sails, anchored, and lowered a dory.

"Looks like my older brother is rowing," said Charlie, "and my sister is in the stern." He waved them onto the ramp.

The workmen had just finished moving and installing the winch engine from the old shed to its new location. Charlie hitched the dory's bow to the cable and up she came.

So much easier, thought Louie. He watched Charlie hug his sister and slap his brother on the back.

"Glad you two came," Charlie commented.

"Can you and your ma and pa join us for dinner while Charlie packs his duffel?" Ma asked Charlie's brother.

Charlie offered to row out to persuade his parents to come ashore while Louie showed his sister and brother around Two Tree Island and the lighthouse tower.

Ma went back up to the house to fix dinner.

"Yer young man's sure a good builder," one of the workmen said to Charlie's ma and pa when he winched up the dory on its return trip. "He helped us build these two sheds."

"Humpf," said Charlie's pa as he examined the buildings, "better he'd stayed at home and helped his pa catch fish."

"I think you did a good job," Charlie's ma quickly added. "Maybe you can fix our broken chairs, now."

"Sure, Ma," Charlie replied ignoring his pa's remarks.

Louie helped Charlie collect his clothes, harmonica, and a carving of Sammy he had made with Louie's help. They stuffed them all in Charlie's duffel.

After dinner, Ma and Louie walked with Charlie and his family to the new boat house. Charlie's brother took turns rowing them out to the anchored *Tipsy*.

Before he climbed into the dory, Charlie turned to Louie's ma and said, "Thanks for everything, M'am."

Then he whispered in her ear, "Especially for not telling."

When he crossed arms with Louie to say goodbye, Louie couldn't stop the tears that streamed down his face. After the dory was stowed on board, the *Tipsy*'s anchor weighed, and her sails set, Louie climbed the lighthouse tower steps to wave to Charlie from the catwalk. Sammy flew from nowhere and perched on the railing by his side.

Ma joined them both. Together they prepared to man the Two Tree Island light for the night.

To order additional copies of

Manning the
LIGHT

Have your credit card ready and call:

1-877-421-READ (7323)

or please visit our web site at
www.pleasantword.com

Also available at: www.amazon.com

Printed in the United States
54425LVS00003B/26